P9-DKD-600

My Miserable Life

My Miserable Life

F. L. BLOCK

illustrated by EDWARD HEMINGWAY

Christy Ottaviano Books
Henry Holt and Company • New York

Henry Holt and Company, LLC
Publishers since 1866
175 Fifth Avenue, New York, New York 10010
mackids.com

Henry Holt® is a registered trademark of Henry Holt and Company, LLC.
Text copyright © 2016 by F. L. Block
Illustrations copyright © 2016 by Edward Hemingway

All rights reserved.

Library of Congress Cataloging-in-Publication Data
Names: Block, Francesca Lia. | Hemingway, Edward, illustrator.
Title: My miserable life / F.L. Block ; illustrated by Edward Hemingway.
Description: First edition. | New York : Henry Holt and Company, 2016. |
Summary: An overprotective mother, an unfriendly older sister,
and a friend-stealing school bully are some of the challenges
faced by thoughtful ten-year-old Ben Hunter of Filmland, California.
Identifiers: LCCN 2015022326 |
ISBN 9780805096286 (hardback) | ISBN 9781627796590 (e-book)
Subjects: | CYAC: Friendship—Fiction. | Schools—Fiction | Family life—California—Fiction. |
California—Fiction. | BISAC: JUVENILE FICTION / Humorous Stories. | JUVENILE FICTION /
Social Issues / Friendship. | JUVENILE FICTION / School & Education.
Classification: LCC PZ7.B61945 My 2016 | DDC [Fic]—dc23
LC record available at http://lccn.loc.gov/2015022326

Our books may be purchased in bulk for promotional, educational, or business use.
Please contact your local bookseller or the Macmillan Corporate and Premium Sales Department
at (800) 221-7945 ext. 5442 or by e-mail at MacmillanSpecialMarkets@macmillan.com.

First Edition—2016 / Designed by April Ward
Printed in the United States of America by R. R. Donnelley & Sons Company,
Harrisonburg, Virginia

1 3 5 7 9 10 8 6 4 2

For S. and J.

SEPTEMBER

ABOUT ME QUESTIONNAIRE
by Ben Hunter

I am a person who is happy when . . . I have friends.

I am a person who is sad when . . . I lose.

My favorite color is . . . red.

My favorite sport is . . . baseball, and my favorite team is the Darters.

My favorite holiday is . . . Halloween (except when my mom, aka the Halloween Fairy, steals my candy).

My favorite animal is . . . Monkeylad. He is part weiner dog but looks part monkey (tail), rabbit (feet: he hops with his back legs), and Rastafarian (ears). He is my favorite, except when he is possessed by a demon or when he steals meat off people's tables. I am trying to teach him to behave better, but he doesn't listen very well.

I live in a place called . . . Filmland, California, where movies are made, as you can tell by the name. Our neighborhood is very safe, but my mom still won't let me ride my bike by myself.

I am a person who likes... sports, running fast, and sugar.

I am a person who dislikes... too-healthy food, stinky sunscreen that my mom forces me to wear, and bullies.

My family is special to me because... they love me even though they are annoying.

My friends are special to me because... they are there for me. Actually, I'm still looking for friends.

Dear Ben,

I have a feeling you will make some nice friends in fifth grade. I look forward to getting to know you better. I'm also a Darters fan. Go Darters! And I love sugar. Maybe I'll make some cupcakes for the class soon. Your dog sounds funny. My cat, Cat's Pajamas, or PJ for short, is part dog, part rat, and part rabbit, too.

Sincerely,

Ms. Washington

CHAPTER 1
MISERABLE

Even though I have a mom who worries too much, a twelve-year-old sister who never stops texting, and a dog named Monkeylad who runs away to steal meat off the neighbors' tables, I really thought things were going to get better for me in fifth grade. But it's the second week, and my life is still pretty miserable.

Things started out okay. This cool kid, Leif

Zuniga, who also likes sports and movies and collecting baseball cards, had been having lunch with me every day.

My mom packed me the usual almond-butter-and-organic-fruit-juice-sweetened-jam-on-whole-wheat-bread sandwich, fresh fruit, carrots, and dried seaweed. Leif took one look at it, said, "Aw, man," and shared his chips and cookies with me, which was awesome. Then we played handball at recess, and we even planned some times to hang out on weekends.

I have a teacher named Ms. Washington, who is supposed to be the nicest teacher in the school, and she sure seems that way so far.

I got A's on my spelling and math tests.

Serena Perl, from kindergarten and first, second, third, and fourth grades, is in my class again. Sometimes I stare at the back of her head because she has this perfectly straight part, and I wonder how she or her mother gets it that way every single day. Her hair, which is the same gold color as her skin, must be pretty long when she takes out the braids. Serena Perl even smiled at me a few times. She has dimples.

At home, my sister, Angelina, was still texting. Monkeylad was still trying to escape. Mom was still being excessively safe. But things were good at school with Ms. Washington, Leif Zuniga, and Serena Perl.

Then, at the end of the second week, everything changed. A new kid came into the classroom. He was a pipsqueak with hair like that singer my sister loves, Dustin Peeper. I recognized him from summer camp.

Rocko Hoggen.

The camp was called 4 Kids Only, so when I first went there, when I was around six, I expected to play with just a few kids. The camp logo even had a picture of just FOUR children. But when Mom dropped me off, there were hundreds of screaming kids.

I told my mom I didn't want to stay because of the false advertising. She asked what I meant, and I told her there were way more than four kids, and she laughed, which made me even madder.

"Don't laugh at me," I said.

"I'm sorry, Ben, but I was laughing with you, not at you."

But I wasn't laughing.

Last summer I had to go back again. On the morning of the first day, my mom packed me a lunch with an almond butter sandwich, fruit, and seaweed. Then she chased me down, waving her bottle of smelly sunscreen that makes my skin look white and streaky. Monkeylad was leaping along behind her. He loves to lick sunscreen off me about as much as my mom loves to put it on.

All *I* wanted to do was stay home and eat sugar and watch TV, but my sister and I aren't allowed to eat sugar on weekdays, and we don't even have TV, only a DVD player, because my mom is a librarian and doesn't believe in television. She makes us read every night, but I'm usually not that interested in the books she brings home for me.

I think she's kind of hypocritical because she sneaks off to the gym almost every day to run on the treadmill and watch bad reality shows. I know this because one of Angelina's friends' dads owns the gym and told Angelina that my mom watches *How to Be a Hottie* and *America's Next OMG*. Without a TV, our house is boring. Which is why, even if I had any friends, they wouldn't come over.

At least I saw someone I knew at camp— Marvin Davis, who was in T-ball with me in kindergarten. He and I hung out at 4 Kids Only and played volleyball, and it was pretty cool.

But the next day, this kid named Rocko Hoggen came to camp. I bet

ROCKO

when you hear a name like that, you think big, burly pit-bull-type kid, not a little poodle. Rocko started talking to Marvin right away. I could tell he was trouble.

Later, Marvin and I were playing soccer and I felt a shove. I fell over onto the grass, and it hurt. I couldn't get up, and then the counselor came and helped me, and Marvin helped, too, and the counselor said he was going to call my mom. I tried not to cry by biting my lip, but my arm hurt like a pit bull had taken a bite out of it. A little

while later, Mom came running into the nurse's office screaming, "Where's my baaaaaby? What happened?" I was so embarrassed that I forgot about how much pain I was in.

"I think he broke his collarbone," the counselor said.

"He what? He broke his collarbone?" yelled my mom. She speaks in question marks when she's upset.

One of the counselors drove us to the hospital, and they X-rayed me and gave me some kind of medicine that made me feel better but also really weird. My mom told me I was saying some goofy things like "The kid that pushed me is a peeper-squeak," but I don't remember. I got a sling for my arm to take pressure off my collarbone, which is actually called a clavicle. I thought I might be able to get out of 4 Kids Only, with a shattered body part and all, but nooooo! I still had to go to camp, but I couldn't run around or play any sports, which made it even worse.

When I got back to camp, I went looking for

Marvin. He was hanging out with the pipsqueak I'd only glimpsed for a second before he'd pushed me down "by accident."

I went up to Marvin to show him my sling, and he said, "Cool," but Rocko didn't say anything. He just tossed his hair like Dustin Peeper and looked away and started humming to himself. Then he said to Marvin, "Come on, let's play handball."

Marvin said, "Do you want to play, Ben?"

But Rocko said, "He can't. He broke his arm, and his bones are fragile."

"Collarbone," I said. I would have said *clavicle*, but I didn't want to sound like a nerd. *(And you actually broke it, pipsqueak.)*

They went off to play, and I sat on a bench by myself. At lunchtime I went to eat with Marvin, and there was Rocko again. I sat with them, and Marvin talked to me, but Rocko didn't say anything. I got up to go to the bathroom, and when I came back, my lunch was gone. I hate my miserable lunches, but I had to eat something. I asked

Marvin if he had seen my lunch, and he said no, he had gone to throw his away, and when he got back, mine wasn't there. I looked at Rocko. He wouldn't look me in the eye. He tossed his hair like Dustin Peeper and turned away. Marvin gave me an extra fruit roll he had in his pocket. Still, I was hungry for the rest of the day.

Rocko Hoggen is the worst bully there is. If there was a word called *worstest*, that would be him. Although my mom would **WORSTEST** die if I used the word *worstest*. She

also hates the word *funnest* **FUNNEST** and when people say *a whole nother thing*. "Is there such a thing as the word *nother*?" she will say. "What is that?"

All summer Rocko was the bane of my existence. My mom would say, "Good use of the word *bane*, Ben." I was just so glad that Rocko was out of my life so I could start the school year fresh.

But there he was again, standing in Ms. Washington's classroom.

CHAPTER 2
THE BANE

I decided to ignore Rocko Hoggen. But at recess, when I went to play handball with Leif, there was the BANE. He blinked at me and tossed his hair.

"Can you play handball?" Rocko asked. "I thought you broke your arm."

"My collarbone," I said. "And it's not broken anymore." *Dork. Jerk. Pipsqueak.*

"Well, Leif and I are playing now," Rocko said, hitting the ball.

I looked at Leif.

Leif looked at me.

I looked harder at him.

Leif shrugged. "Rocko lives next door to me," he said. "Our moms are best friends. So are our dads. Since we were born."

"We were born in the same hospital on the same day," Rocko added, slamming the pink rubber ball against the wall with his little grimy pipsqueak hands. "Kind of like twins."

I, on the other hand, was born in a bathtub at a birthing center. I didn't have a best friend being born at the same time. I don't even have a dad, since my mom used a donor to have Angelina and me.

When I got home from school, my mom noticed that something was wrong. I know this because she kept asking, "What's wrong, Ben? What's wrong, sweetie?" I wouldn't tell her. How are you supposed to explain to your worried-looking mom that your life is irrevocably miserable? (Even my correct use of the word *irrevocably* would not comfort her.) But when I started throwing my favorite baseball cards, my mom put her arms around me and made me tell her what was going on.

"Rocko Hoggen is in my class," I said.

"That kid from 4 Kids Only?"

"That pipsqueak from One Zillion Kids Only, who broke my clavicle," I said.

"It was an accident, sweetie." I could tell by my mom's squeaky-sounding voice that if I insisted that it wasn't an accident, she would call Rocko's house and make him apologize.

So I just said, "Yeah, but I hate him. And now he's trying to steal Leif Zuniga." I hadn't meant to say that about Leif Zuniga, but it just came out.

Angelina walked in not wearing her headphones, for once. She had on shiny white leather high-top sneakers, cut-off shorts things that she rolled up when she left the house in the morning and rolled down when she got home, a football jersey with shiny gold numbers, and a gold chain around her neck. She has millions of different outfits with lots of what she calls "bling" on them; I pretty much would wear the same Darters baseball jersey and shorts every day if I could.

"Is that the kid you've been hanging out with?" she asked.

I nodded. I told them the whole story about the handball game and how Rocko and Leif had been best friends since they were newborns in the hospital, spitting up on each other while their moms, who were also best friends, envisioned their sons' futures together.

"Maybe you could find another friend in your class to play with?" Mom said.

"It's 'hang out with,' Mom, not play. He's in fifth grade now," said Angelina. She went over to the refrigerator and pointed to the paper whale I had made in second grade that said FRIENDSHIP MEANS TRUSTING EACH OTHER. It bugs me that my mom still keeps that up.

I appreciated that Angelina had corrected my

mom about not using the word *play*, but there was no one else I wanted to hang out with. Simon Heller picks his nose and sticks it under his desk. Joe Knapp is only eight and a half and just reads all day. Nicholas Gonzalez never sits still or stops talking. Darby Levine has a Mohawk and hangs out with eighth graders. And for some inexplicable reason, EVERY SINGLE OTHER KID IN MY CLASS OF TWENTY-FIVE IS A GIRL!

"People usually don't realize they're being rude. They're just thinking about themselves. You need to go where the love is, Ben Hunter. Like with Serena Perl, maybe?" Since Angelina got her braces off, she always flashes her perfect teeth at me. I still have some baby teeth and two front chompers that you can see a mile away. "Come here, Monkeylad," she called, putting on some fresh lip gloss.

Monkeylad trotted in, and she picked him up. His tail was sticking through the hole in the back of the cheerleader outfit he was wearing. The costume belonged to a bear Angelina had made herself at Stuff-It, and she liked to put it on Monkeylad since she was a cheerleader, too.

Our dog is obsessed with lip gloss and tried to lick it off Angelina, but she moved her head away.

"See?" Angelina said. "That's what I mean, right, Monkeyladdy? Go where the love is." She winked at me. "He's a real chick magnet. You should bring him to school one day for show-and-tell."

Show-and-tell? That was worse than using the word *play*. And the only chicks Monkeylad could get would be cooked chickens stolen from some-one else's table!

Some evenings at dinnertime, Monkeylad manages to escape. At first we thought he was running away, but then we heard our neighbor Mrs. Finkelstein knocking on the door and yell-ing, "Your baby's home!" She was standing there with Monkeylad, who had something in his mouth. It looked like a mummy head or something really gross, but it was actually a fully cooked Easter ham.

We had no idea how he got it. But then he kept running away and coming back with different things in his mouth—pot roasts and turkeys and chickens and steaks.

For obvious reasons, the neighbors don't like us very much. Especially Mrs. Finkelstein and a man we call the Grump. The Grump lives alone. He puts on a suit and tie and goes to work every day and comes home and never seems to leave his house any other time or speak to anyone. When my mom tries to ask him his name, he just turns his back on her and walks away. When the Grump and Mrs. Finkelstein see Monkeylad come running, they slam their doors, but sometimes he gets in through the windows. Then they come over and yell at us, and my mom has to buy them a new pot roast or whatever.

THE GRUMP

Angelina put her headset back on and walked out of the room with Monkeylad. I wished she'd leave the dog with me for once. I never get to sleep with him.

Monkeylad came from the shelter. My sister and I had been begging my mom for another dog after our perfect, beautiful, well-behaved golden-doodle, Pleasant, got very sick and had to be put to sleep. My mom would say, "How can I have another dog? I'm so busy I could hardly take care of Pleasant," and my sister would say, "You took good care of her, Mom. Until the part where you KILLED her!" I guess the guilt trip finally worked, because we got Monkeylad.

At first Monkeylad seemed like a little angel. He sat quietly on his bed, staring up at us with puppy eyes, or pranced down the street on his walks like a show dog. But then one day it was like he had become possessed by a demon.

For no reason, he started running in mad circles around the house growling. My mom tried to catch him, but he bared his teeth, and his eyes rolled back in his head and turned blue. When she finally caught him and put him in the bad room, aka the bathroom, to calm down, he nipped at her shoelaces until he untied them with his teeth.

We have to put him in the bad room every so often. When he comes out, Angelina takes a photo of him and posts it on Fastpic with her other photographs. She captions the picture "Bad Dog Photo." Sometimes she takes really blurry, badly lit shots of him and uses the same caption as a joke.

Monkeylad becomes possessed by a demon about once a month. We still have no idea why. Maybe he was traumatized as a puppy in the shelter.

When the demon calms down, Monkeylad looks guilty for a few minutes, but after that he seems to think pretty highly of himself. He won't obey me. Maybe I could learn something from him. I do everything everyone tells me, but I always feel like I'm doing something wrong.

THE THIRD WEEK OF FIFTH GRADE

by Ben Hunter

My week has been miserable.

I know we're supposed to support our opening statement (why I am having a miserable week) with at least three examples. Here they are:

Rocko Hoggen is in my class.

Rocko Hoggen steals my friends. So far he has stolen Marvin Davis and Leif Zuniga.

Rocko Hoggen broke my clavicle.

Those are the reasons I am having a miserable week.

Dear Ben,

I'm sorry you are having a miserable week. You can always hand me a little note if you are feeling left out or uncomfortable. I don't think Rocko means any harm. I asked him about what happened, and he said that when you broke your arm at camp, he was really worried about you and that the boys were sad you couldn't play handball. He just likes to be friends with Leif, since they've known each other for so long. Why don't you try being friends with Simon, Joe, Darby, or Nicholas? Joe is especially nice. Maybe you could help him come out of his shell and play a little ball. Also, maybe in your next essay, you could try to write about at least one thing that is going okay. It might be a challenge, but I know you can do it.

Ms. Washington

CHAPTER 3
THE CAT'S MEOW

Even though Rocko lied about feeling bad about my clavicle and told Ms. Washington it was my arm because he doesn't even know what a clavicle is, I was feeling a little better after reading Ms. Washington's note. Also, today she gave us chocolate cupcakes that she baked herself. My mom never makes cupcakes anymore.

When I was in second grade, she surprised me by bringing cupcakes to school. Usually she made fruit-juice-sweetened banana nut muffins, but this time she'd promised to behave like a normal mother and bring cupcakes with swirly frosting from the market. She came in, smiling like crazy and wearing bright-colored yoga pants. Her hair was kind of messy, and she was carrying two huge pink boxes. She put the cupcakes on the table. My teacher at the time, Mrs. Kunkel, told me to hand them out. But when I opened the box, I saw that there were these little toy things on top of the cupcakes. You know, those little plastic things that you get at the dentist's or doctor's after they've tortured you for a few minutes with sharp instruments? (As if this makes anything better.)

The toys would have been fine, except some had little pink Hey! Bunny Rabbits! like the ones on my sister's pajamas, and some had blue Timmy the Trains with smiley faces. And all of them were rings that you were supposed to wear on your finger. How would the kids in my class know that I didn't request pink rabbit heads and baby trains on my cupcakes?

I mean, I hadn't been into the smiley trains since kindergarten, when I used to squat on the floor and hop about like a frog trying to move the trains around the track. Then someone discovered lead paint on a few of the trains and my mom got rid of all of them.

Angelina said that my mom had wasted all that money on those poison trains because she never could say no to me because I used to be so cute. I'd put my arms up when I wanted to be held and say, "Hum peas," which meant "Hold me, please."

"Not so cute anymore, dude," Angelina said. "But then you had these fat cheeks and tiny teeth instead of those big honkers, and you smelled like strawberries and not like dirt."

Sometimes I hate my sister more than usual.

In second grade I was still kind of cute, if you ask me, but maybe not cute enough for my mom not to ask me first before she bought cupcakes with stupid girly and babyish plastic rings on them.

I took one look at the cupcakes and started to cry. Mrs. Kunkel was the kind of teacher who believed no one should cry, especially boys. Once she had taken me aside to explain that if boys cried, everyone would make fun of them and label them a crybaby. But I was only seven. I really don't think it's so bad for boys to cry, even when they get older. I especially don't think there's anything wrong with crying when your mom brings babyish cupcakes to school.

Yeah, that's my cupcake story. But Ms. Washington's cupcakes tasted great, and there weren't any stupid plastic toys on them, and even if there had been, no one would have associated them with me.

But today when Ms. Washington was handing out the cupcakes, Rocko Hoggen jumped up, bowed (yes, bowed), and said, "I'll help you distribute the cupcakes, Ms. Washington."

I wanted to help her, but I had been staring at

Serena Perl's part and the little red sparkly things along the neckline of her shirt and hadn't thought of it. Ms. Washington said, "Thank you, Rocko. You are the cat's meow."

Great. Even Ms. Washington was going over to Rocko's side.

Leif Zuniga's mom, who is the room parent, came into the classroom to help Ms. Washington collect and grade the tests. A lady walked in with her. She had on a pink T-shirt with a heart that said RUN FOR YOUR LIFE, just like Mrs. Zuniga's T-shirt.

"Boys and girls, you know our room parent, Mrs. Zuniga," Ms. Washington said. "And this is our other room parent, Mrs. Hoggen. Thank you so much, ladies."

My mother would never be a room parent; she was always too busy for some reason. I guess it's hard being a single mom without a dad to help, but she should have thought of that a long time ago.

My mother didn't even have time to run for

anyone's life. I was glad she wasn't a room parent, because she would have embarrassed me. But still, why couldn't I have a mom who helped Ms. Washington?

Mrs. Zuniga and Mrs. Hoggen seemed like they might hold hands when they left the classroom together; they looked like they really were best friends. Just like their kids.

At recess I ran around the track by myself until I could hardly breathe and felt like throwing up. Maybe I didn't have any friends; maybe my mom wasn't room parent material. I wasn't the cat's pajamas like Rocko. But at least I was fast.

When I got home from school, I guess I looked pretty upset, because my mom was all "What's wrong, Ben? Ben, sweetie? What is it?"

I wouldn't answer.

"Maybe you're hungry? Are you hungry? Did you eat your lunch? Why don't you eat your lunch?" There she went with the question marks again.

"Mom, I hate what you pack me."

She looked through my lunchbox and found the untouched sandwich and seaweed and carrots  and mostly untouched grapes. "How can you go a whole day on three grapes?"

"That's not what's bothering me. Everything is not always about food. You don't know how to parent."

I learned this line from Angelina. It always makes my mom really mad, probably because it's kind of true. She always tells us that no one can make you mad if what they say isn't true, because then it can't hit a nerve. I guess I hit a nerve.

"How could you say that? After all I do for you every day of your life? Do you ever think about all the things I do for you?" She went on and on while I took off my shoes and picked the lint from between my toes, ignoring her.

Angelina came into the room with her cheer-leader friends Twinkle Knoll and Amanda Panda Rodriguez. They were listening to the Nananna song "Na Na Na Na Na Na Na" on Angelina's phone. "What's wrong, Ben?" she asked.

I wouldn't answer her, especially in front of Twinkle and Amanda Panda.

"Remember to go where the love is," my sister said, before dancing away.

But I didn't really know where that was anymore.

Later, I got in bed and my mom came to say good night. "I'm sorry I got so mad," she said.

I told her I was sorry for saying she didn't know how to parent.

"I probably got mad because it's kind of true sometimes. It's a pretty hard job, and I try to do my best, but it's not always very good. Do you want to tell me what happened at school today?"

But I didn't want to tell her. It would have sounded stupid to say, "I'm upset because my teacher called Rocko Hoggen the cat's meow." And my mom would have just said, "I think you're the cat's meow," which wasn't the same thing as Ms. Washington saying it.

Besides, there were so many other things that were wrong, it was kind of overwhelming.

When my mom kissed me and turned off the light, I remembered what Ms. Washington had said about how she wanted me to think of one thing that was okay. I thought for a while. It was September, and not much good stuff happens in September. Summer ends, and you have to go back to school. Then I realized that Halloween was coming in a month. It felt like forever, but at least it was something to look forward to. Sort of.

OCTOBER

THE CANDY CORN CARNIVAL

by Ben Hunter

There's a carnival at our school just before
Halloween to raise money to buy computers and
art supplies. It's called the Candy Corn Carnival.
I'm not sure if I think this is such a good event.

There are many delicious temptations that
I'm not allowed to eat because my mother is an
antisugar fanatic. It doesn't seem fair that my

mom lets me go to an event named after a candy but hardly lets me eat anything sweet.

Another reason I don't like the carnival is the cakewalk. A cakewalk is where they play music and you walk in circles until the music stops. If you're on the number they call when you stop, you win a cake.

My sister, Angelina, won a cake during a Dustin Peeper song called "I Love You, Baby, You Pretty Little Girl." She thought she'd won because Dustin Peeper is good luck for her. The cake was big and pink and white. She gave it to Amanda Panda for safekeeping.

I won a cake, too, during a hip-hop song by the rapper Valet. It was a good song and a good cake. The cake was small and chocolate and beautiful. I loved that cake. True story. But my mom came over just as I won it and asked if she could donate my cake to the homeless shelter. I said no. No way. That cake was mine. I backed away from her and tripped, and my cake fell in the mud. Just then, a kid I know, whose name I will not mention here (but it rhymes with *taco*), walked by and tossed his Dustin Peeper hair and smiled at me.

He said, "Hey, Ben, nice cake."

When we got home, Amanda Panda came over with a big box that she said was for a school project. I knew what was really in there. She and my sister ate it all without sharing any with me.

These are the reasons that I think the Candy Corn Carnival is a bad event and should be abolished.

CHAPTER 4

THE MONSTER HEAD THAT DIDN'T SPURT BLOOD

"**M**om, Ben needs a good Halloween costume," Angelina said. "That will cheer him up. A really scary one, not one for babies. Right, Ben?"

I didn't want to admit that she was right. But it wasn't a bad idea. I had been asking my mom for a Halloween costume for weeks, and Mom just kept saying that I should wear one of my old ones. These included the Timmy the Train that I wore for three years straight, a Ninja Rabbit, and a robot. None of these were acceptable, not to mention that they were all too small. But of course Angelina had an ulterior motive. "Can Monkeylad and I get one?" she asked with a head roll and jump in the air. Twinkle and Amanda Panda, who were with her as usual, followed suit.

My mom rubbed her temples. "Can you and Monkeylad get one, too?" she said in her usual stressed, question-mark way. But she agreed as long as Angelina took me.

Great, I had to go costume shopping with my sister? But at least she'd gotten my mom to fork over the money.

Monkeylad came skidding across the wood floor and jumped up, trying to lick off Angelina's freshly applied lip gloss. He had demon eyes. Angelina and her friends ran away from him, screaming.

My mom asked me to throw a ball with Monkeylad in the backyard, but I didn't want to when his eyes were rolling around like that.

———

Angelina didn't like taking me costume shopping, but she did like to go to Bull's Eye, our favorite neighborhood store, especially when she had cash from Mom. We went straight to the Halloween section. It was well picked through, but among the stupid animal suits and pirates and wizards and vampires that Angelina said were "totally uncool," I saw the perfect costume.

It was a monster with a head that had been split in half so that part of the brain showed. Blood squirted out and ran down the inside of the mask when you squeezed this attached pump. The chest had been split open to reveal a large, bleeding plastic heart. The costume was SICK! I knew I had to have it. But by the time Angelina bought her pink catsuit with ears and tail, there was only enough money to get a monster head that looked like the cool one except it didn't squirt blood.

"You owe me, Ben Hunter," she said. "I got Mom to get you a new costume, and she made me take you instead of going with Twinkle and Amanda Panda. Plus, before you were born, I didn't have to share my costume money with anyone."

So I had to settle, as usual. Monkeylad didn't get a costume at all, but we figured he wouldn't really care that much and he could wear his hot-dog bun from a few years ago.

Angelina likes to play the older-sibling-who-didn't-used-to-have-to-share card. Sometimes it makes me feel bad that I came along and ruined her life. This time it made me mad, because 1) this wasn't her money, it was Mom's, and 2) when Angelina was one and two years old, she couldn't have really cared about how much her tiny pumpkin and Hey! Bunny Rabbit! Halloween costumes cost. Still, I let her get away with her shenanigans this time because if I were her, I would probably resent having me as a little brother, too.

The story goes, when I was born, Angelina

was really mad at my mom and me. Mom bought Angelina a purple teddy bear and had my grandma give it to her and say it was from me. That didn't fool my sister. She knew that a new-born baby can't go out and buy a teddy bear.

When my mother brought me home, Angelina took one look at me and ran outside holding a plastic spoon. My mom followed her and took the spoon away. Angelina had bitten off a piece of it. My mom freaked out and made sure there weren't any pieces of spoon in Angelina's mouth. Then she asked why Angelina was so upset.

"I'm having a hard time, Mommy," two-year-old Angelina said. "I'm afraid the baby will take you away from me." She had started speaking in long sentences when she was nine months old. I, on the other hand, took a long time to speak. Mostly I just liked to listen to my sister. Since we didn't have TV, she was the best entertainment I could get.

My mom tried to comfort Angelina, but my

sister never seemed to have recovered from the trauma of me being born. She would pull my shirts up and poke my fat belly, saying, "Touch, baby! Touch! Touch!" When my mom told her to stop, she said she was just trying to teach me words. No wonder it took me so long to talk.

CHAPTER 5

THE HALLOWEEN FAIRY IS EVIL

The night after the Candy Corn Carnival, I heard shouting and knocking. I went to the door and looked through the peephole. The Grump from next door was standing there. Monkeylad was next to him with something gross in his mouth.

"That dog stole my cake," said the Grump. "This is the last straw. If you don't do something about that dog, I will call the authorities."

"I'm so sorry, Mr. . . . ," my mom said. I didn't

feel so bad about calling him the Grump if she didn't even know his name.

I felt like a Grump, too. Monkeylad had tried to help me, but I couldn't eat that piece of cake he'd brought. It had dog teeth marks all over it.

Angelina and her friends were going to have a Halloween party at Twinkle Knoll's house. Twinkle Knoll has five brothers and sisters who all look just like her, each one year older and one head taller than the next, with big, perfectly round blue eyes and long blond hair.

Their parents let them have parties, watch TV all the time, and eat as much candy as they want. Obviously their house is a perfect place to hang out at on Halloween. There's no so-called Halloween Fairy there to steal your hard-earned Halloween candy. Not like at my house, where she lurks in the corners, ready and waiting with her dreaded Lurning Bush school-supply store gift certificates to trade for your candy.

First of all, you can't make up for stolen candy

with school supplies, and second of all, why would you misspell the name of a place where kids were supposed to go to learn? The little buddies would get confused. And what did that name mean, anyway?

Just then, my mom came out of her room wearing THE WINGS.

One Halloween she'd dressed up as a fairy with these big wings that looked like the feathers came from real pigeons, a wreath of fake pink flowers on her head, and an old lace dress that kept getting tangled and torn on the branches when she took me out trick-or-treating. She had to turn sideways to let the kids pass her on the sidewalk because the wings were so huge. One year she was an angel wearing the same wings. One year she was a butterfly. Yep, same pigeon-feather wings.

And this year she had on an orange-and-black outfit with orange-and-black-striped stockings and the same wings.

"Guess who I am?" my mom asked.

She was the Halloween Fairy, but I couldn't bring myself to say it.

"Are you ready?"

I didn't want to go trick-or-treating with her, but it would have been worse to stay home and give out candy to Rocko Hoggen and Leif Zuniga and Serena Perl, who were probably all trick-or-treating together dressed in matching zombie outfits. So I made my mom promise to keep her distance and pretend she wasn't with me if we ran into anyone I knew.

Before we left, Monkeylad was having one of his demon possessions. His eyes were rolling up in his head and had turned blue.

"We need to exercise the demon so he doesn't attack trick-or-treaters at the door," I told my mom.

"You mean exorcise?" she said, laughing.

"That's what I said," I said.

She bent down really slowly, holding out a Chix Stix treat, caught Monkeylad, and Velcroed on his hot-dog bun. As soon as it was on, he sat down and looked up at her with twinkling black puppy eyes. It was like magic.

"This hot-dog bun was worth the investment," my mom said. Monkeylad had worn it a few times already, but it was harder to put on now since he'd gotten a little chubby around the middle.

I had to admit, he did look kind of cute as a hot dog. And it would be much harder for him to escape and steal meat while wearing that thing.

Our neighborhood was lit up with orange jack-o'-lantern lights, and there were vats of dry ice and dangling skeletons and blow-up witches and cobwebs getting caught over my mouth, and it was all pretty cool, in spite of my mom's wings and my dog in his too-small bun.

As I was walking along the street, I saw Joe Knapp from school. Joe Knapp wears big glasses with thick lenses. His name is embroidered on his jackets and his backpack. His lunch box and backpack match; they are both in the shape of books. So I wasn't surprised to see that for Halloween he was dressed as a dictionary. His dad was dressed as a giant baby in fuzzy footsie pajamas. I didn't feel as embarrassed about my mom's wings after that. Joe waved to me but then ducked his head, maybe when he realized that I was looking at his dad.

I filled a pillowcase with candy and was really excited to go home and eat some. I figured my mom might be nicer this year, because of all the hardship I had recently endured, and maybe let me eat a few extra pieces and keep the rest for the following weekends. Actually, if we followed her two-pieces-per-weekend rule, the candy would last me for a year's worth of weekends. I could almost taste the hard sugar crackling against my teeth and the chocolate melting on my tongue.

But when we got home, Mom said, "Time for the Halloween Fairy."

I looked at her with dread.

"You can keep three pieces for tonight, okay?" she added, smiling like she was doing me a big favor.

"Seriously, Mom? Seriously? You've got to be kidding me, Mom?" I was so upset I was talking in question marks like she did.

"Okay, would you like five pieces? The Halloween Fairy will give you a gift certificate if you leave her the rest, okay, Ben?" She picked up a basket she'd set by the door. "Would you like an apple?"

Hadn't she heard that you can't give out apples for Halloween? No one in their right mind gave out apples! I had barely eaten any candy, and I felt like I was going to throw up.

I was trying not to cry.

"What five pieces do you want, Ben?" my mom asked.

I picked the biggest candy bars and stuffed them into my mouth. I didn't even enjoy them. The whole night was ruined.

And if you think that was bad, wait till you hear what happened next. The doorbell rang, and my mom ran to answer it. She was holding the apple basket, and her wings were getting caught on furniture and dripping feathers everywhere. Monkeylad was following her in his hot-dog bun. I heard her talking to the kids at the door, and then she called out, "Ben, can you come here?"

I don't know why I did it. I was like a robot. I walked slowly toward the door, and there were three trick-or-treaters standing on the step. There was a boy dressed as a werewolf, a girl dressed as a vampire with tiny plastic fangs and a red velvet cape, and a kid with the same costume as mine. Only better. It was the version with the beating, bleeding heart and the blood that spurted out and dripped down the mask face when you squeezed the pump. And the kid? It was Rocko Hoggen. He was with Leif Zuniga and Serena Perl.

"Hi, Ben," Serena said. She had glitter around

her eyes, and it sparkled in the porch light. "I didn't know you lived here. Your dog is cute. Are you okay?"

"Hey," I said, looking down at my feet, away from her glitter eyes, away from her dimples, away from her braids, away from her fangs.

A cop came up behind them. He was over six feet tall and bald. "Excuse me, ma'am, are you handing out apples to these kids?"

My mom took a step back and almost dropped the apple basket.

The man laughed and adjusted his black stretch pants. "Just kidding. I'm not really a cop. But some kids are going to use the apples to bomb cars. You really can't give out apples on Halloween anymore," he said.

"Well, at least they're healthy," my mom said. "You gave me a little scare there. I think our kids know each other?"

"I'm Peter Hoggen," the cop said. "Nice to meet you."

My mom shook his hand and smiled. "I'm

Ben's mom," she said. "Basically I just go by that now. Ben's Mom. Angelina's Mom."

"Looks like our boys have the same costume, Ben's Mom," Peter Hoggen said. "Almost."

Rocko pressed the button that made his heart light up and seep blood.

Was I in a bad monster movie? Was I in ten-year-old-boy hell? No, I was in my own miserable life.

"Are you sure you don't want an apple?" my mom asked.

The cop had already walked away, waving his hand over his head and chuckling to himself. "An apple a day doesn't keep the cops away on Halloween."

"Uh, that's okay," Rocko said to my mom's apple. "Our bags are kind of full. Bye, Ben. Nice costume. Hope that cakewalk cake was good."

"Bye, Ben," said Leif Zuniga. "See you in class."

Serena Perl looked back at me and flashed her little fangs with a worried look in her eyes before she disappeared into the fog that had crept up like a ghost.

I ran into the bathroom and looked at myself. My eyes showed through the mask. The eyeliner Angelina had applied to make me look scarier was streaked from my tears. And Serena Perl had seen.

My mom tried to talk to me while I lay in bed with the sheet over my face.

"Are you a ghost?" she said.

I didn't answer.

"Should we cut out some eyes so you can be a ghost?"

I threw the sheet off. "I told you I'm not five years old anymore, Mom."

"I'm sorry," she said. "I know you're too old to believe in the Halloween Fairy. That's why I dressed up as her, because it's part of the joke. And I'm sorry I gave out apples, too. I promise I won't do that again."

I didn't say anything back to her.

"But I still don't want you to eat too much candy."

Now I really wasn't going to speak.

In the morning there was a piece of paper under my pillow. Guess what it was? A gift certificate to the Lurning Bush school-supply store. There were a few pigeon feathers scattered on the sheet beside it.

NOVEMBER

MY MISSION STATEMENT
by Ben Hunter

Did you know that early Californians lived in mud huts and that missions were their first real buildings? Missions are interesting to me for several reasons.

Since building my own mission, I've learned how difficult they must have been to build. My mom took me to the Lurning Bush, and we bought Popsicle sticks and sticky white clay. The clay kept sticking to my fingers and not the Popsicle sticks. I wonder if the people who built the missions had this much trouble.

Another reason missions are interesting is that the people who built them wanted to be self-sufficient. They had to produce crops and maintain livestock and develop their own water systems.

For me, being self-sufficient is serving myself cold cereal and milk when my mom has an early-morning meeting and can't force me to eat oatmeal. So I think self-sufficiency is good. Sometimes I imagine what it would be like to run away and be entirely self-sufficient. I would eat candy on weekdays, run through sprinklers in the morning instead of taking showers, and hang out with stray cats if I needed company. But I guess I would miss my mom and my sister and especially my dog, even though he gets demon eyes.

A third reason missions are interesting is

that they were built close enough together so people could use them as rest stops on long trips. My family and I went on a long camping trip two summers ago, and we had to stop at rest stops. When you have one mom, two kids, and a dog, someone has to pee pretty often. Bathrooms at rest stops usually smell bad. My sister complained that there weren't any mirrors for her to look at herself or hot water to wash with or paper towels to dry her hands. My sister would not have done very well in mission days.

CHAPTER 6

AN IMPOSSIBLE MISSION

After I turned in my report, I learned more about missions. I learned from Ms. Washington that the Native Americans didn't just learn how to build big fancy whitewashed adobe buildings with tiled roofs overnight. They were conquered by the Spanish, who then tried to convert them to Christianity and made them work really hard at the missions.

My mission didn't come out very well, but I was still proud of it, since I made it without a kit.

Angelina had told me that when she was in fifth grade, her class had to make missions and everyone except her used a kit. She got the best grade because hers was handmade.

When I arrived at school, I saw a playhouse-sized building standing in the middle of the classroom. It had a red roof, real glass windows, and a bell tower.

Rocko Hoggen stood at the entrance, ushering people inside. Only three kids could fit at a time, so the rest of the class lined up, trying to get back

in again, except for Joe Knapp, who was sitting cross-legged on the floor reading. He looked up through his dorky glasses for a second and wiggled his fingers in the air at me in what might have been a wave.

"Hey, Ben," Rocko said. "You want a turn? Can I see your mission?"

I wanted to hide it behind my back. It was a gooey blob. Some of the clay hadn't stuck to the Popsicle sticks, and they were showing through. I backed away, and the mission slid off the piece of cardboard I'd put it on and fell onto the floor. Ms. Washington helped me pick it up.

"You did a good job, Ben," she said while we were crouched on the ground together. She smelled like butter, cocoa powder, and sugar. "I see you made it all by yourself."

Unlike *some* people, I thought.

I looked up from my broken mission to see Serena Perl; she was ringing the real bell in Rocko's bell tower.

When I got home from school, I went into my closet and took out my SECRET BOX. It has all the things that are important to me, like ticket stubs from the Darters baseball games my mom used to take me to before money got tight, my straight-A report cards, and some pictures of me playing baseball and eating ice cream cones with my mom.

Those were the good old days, before my mom was stressed out and worried so much. I moved everything aside and took out what I was looking for. It was a red paper heart with puppy stickers and glitter writing (she has always been all about the sparkle) that said I LOVE YOU BEN HUNTER. It was a valentine from Serena Perl from kindergarten.

There had been a time, before Rocko Hoggen existed to me, before he broke my clavicle and it had to fuse itself back together again (probably unevenly), before I lost my baby curls and got big front teeth, a time when Serena Perl said she loved me. Now it was all over. Forever. My mission had failed.

WHAT I AM GRATEFUL FOR
by Ben Hunter

I am grateful for many things. Well, some things. Well, three things.

I am grateful for the Darters because they are a good team, and they are my team, and my mom used to take me to see them play. Because it was a special occasion, my mom let me eat Darter Dogs, frozen lemonade, and ice cream, and I explained each play to her.

I am grateful for my teacher, Ms. Washington, because she is the best teacher ever. She pays attention, listens, and understands.

I am grateful for my grandmother for not being afraid to put her hands inside a turkey, for putting marshmallows on yams, for not using the word *bad* except in extreme situations, and for playing ball with me.

These are the things I am grateful for.
But sometimes I forget.

Dear Ben,

I'm grateful to have you in my class.

Happy Thanksgiving,

Ms. Washington

CHAPTER 7
GRATEFUL FOR GRANNY

Thanksgiving is a pretty good holiday. There isn't an endless supply of candy that you aren't allowed to eat. There is pumpkin pie, which you can eat because it is technically a vegetable. Best of all, my grandma, Minnie, always comes from Date Palm Oasis to celebrate with us.

My grandma is super cool. She has more energy than any old person I know, even more energy than my mom. Grandma

GRANDMA hikes and swims every day. She never gets mad at me, and she lets me talk to her about sports for hours and doesn't get bored. She says, "Ben, the way you reel off those Darters statistics is really impressive. I think we have a genius on our hands."

One time I got to visit her in Date Palm Oasis all by myself. She lives in a little cabin boat on a lake in the middle of the date palms. You have to walk on a swaying bridge to get to it—so cool! Rabbits play and roadrunners run on the banks of the lake at dawn. My grandma's house is filled with games that she actually plays with me and a TV and my favorite DVDs, and she makes me breakfast for dinner. She says she enjoys living in the desert because the air is better and there isn't any traffic, but I think she just likes to have a little distance between herself and my mom.

This Thanksgiving she drove in from the desert and ran back and forth from her car unloading everything, kissing me each time she came inside. "Oh, Ben, you are so wonderful. You are the most adorable young man I have ever seen." She brought these scented candles that smelled like apple pie and pumpkin pie, and bouquets of orange and yellow and red flowers, and all these pots and pans and serving dishes and groceries. My mom gets grossed out by cooking turkeys, but my grandma just reached right inside that bird and pulled out all the innards and whistled while she did it. And she made mashed potatoes with lots of butter and cream, and yams topped with marshmallows, and pumpkin pie.

But on Thanksgiving night, my family were up to their old tricks.

"Oh, Mom, why did you put marshmallows on the yams? Aren't they plenty sweet as it is?" my mom said to my grandma.

My grandmother continued to merrily scoop yams with marshmallows onto my plate. "It's a special occasion! And besides, it might get them

to eat some vegetables. Vitamin A! Would you like some, Angelina?"

"No thanks, Grandma. Yams make me vomit," Angelina said. She sipped her mineral water.

"Angelina!" my mom said. "Is that a way to talk at dinner?"

"Well, it's true."

Then I heard the sound of a Lady Blah-Blah song, very softly coming from under the table. Angelina was receiving a text, even though she wasn't allowed to have her phone at dinner, but I saw, and before I could tell, she started crying.

"What's wrong, sweetheart?" my grandma asked.

"Amanda Panda sent me a link about the brutal treatment of Native Americans by the Pilgrims. This is a barbaric holiday," she said. She got up and ran out of the room. I think it was just because she hates green beans and yams, even with marshmallows on top.

A little while later, my grandma announced that there was pie with vanilla ice cream, and Angelina came back in. She didn't seem too upset anymore. Just as we were going to eat dessert, there was a commotion in the bushes outside the window and Monkeylad leaped inside onto the table, whisking his tail through the gravy bowl. In his smiling mouth was what looked like an alien baby. Angelina clutched her stomach and ran out again, saying she was going to vomit. My mom screamed after Angelina not to keep using the word *vomit* at the dinner table, and she screamed at Monkeylad that he was a bad dog.

My grandma said you shouldn't call anyone *bad* because there was no such thing as bad except for Hitler and racists and terrorists and murderers and global warming. And then, of course, there was a knock on the door and it was our neighbor Mrs. Finkelstein.

"That animal of yours stole my Cornish hen," she shrieked.

She was wearing a flowered housedress and was bent almost in two over her cane.

"Oh, I'm so sorry," my grandma said. "Come in and have some dinner with us. I guess Monkeylad was just trying to invite you over in his own special way. I'm so sorry about your hen, but we have lots of turkey and pie."

She guided Mrs. Finkelstein inside, sat her down, and prepared a plate for her while Monkeylad skulked under the table because he had been called bad, as in global warming and Hitler, when he only wanted to give my mom an alien baby as a present.

"Hey," I said when we were finished, "why don't we all go outside and throw the ball?"

"I have to do the dishes," my mom said. "Look how many of them there are. Maybe afterward."

Grandma and Monkeylad were walking Mrs. Finkelstein home, and Angelina had already disappeared into her room.

I really wished I had someone to play ball with. Or someone to watch football with in a dark Man Room that smelled of potato chips and dirty socks. Instead I had to walk around the backyard in circles, throwing the ball in the air and reciting baseball stats.

"Ben?"

I turned around. It was my grandma, standing under a tree that blooms red flowers in the spring.

"Would you like me and Monkeylad to play ball with you?" She is really short, with eyes that crinkle up when she smiles. She always wears pink, and she has pink tortoiseshell glasses that turn up at the corners and have little sparkles on them. She looks like a storybook grandma. And she can throw a ball, too, my granny. Monkeylad caught it in his mouth.

"You're a good dog, Monkeylad," Grandma said. He seemed very proud.

DECEMBER

CHAPTER 8
THURSDAY IS CRAZY

Not only did we have to stay at home for winter break instead of going on a vacation like a normal family, but my mom's friend's daughter came to stay with us.

"Why does she get my room?" I yelped when I found out.

"Why does he have to stay with me?" screamed Angelina.

"I'm really sorry, you guys, but Amy's having a hard time, and she needs some help. We have to show her how a happy family functions." There were no question marks, so we knew my mom wasn't going to back down. "Besides, she was the cutest little girl. I haven't seen her in years, but when I held her in my arms and she called me Aunty, that was when I knew I wanted kids of my own."

But things had changed. Amy was not a cute little girl anymore. In fact, she was not a normal person.

Thursday

"Hi. You must be Amy?" my mom said when the person with black hair and black clothes and black boots with spikes came to the door.

Angelina ran to pick up Monkeylad so he wouldn't get hurt from the spikes.

"Hey. It's Thursday," said the person.

"Thursday? Isn't it Monday?" said my mom.

"No. My name. It's Thursday."

"Your name is Thursday?"

The person rolled her eyes, which were lined with black stuff. "I was born on a Thursday. Every Thursday I feel like hell and want to die."

"Then why did you name yourself after that day?" Angelina asked.

The person ignored her. She glared at me. "Don't you have a day of the week you hate?"

"Sunday," I said.

"What day were you born?"

I looked at my mom. "Sunday?" she said sheepishly.

"See? I rest my case. Where do I sleep?" the person said.

I felt an invisible baseball slam into my gut as the truth fully hit me: I was getting kicked out of my room.

Our scary guest stomped away in her spike-studded black boots.

"I can't believe this," I said.

Angelina stomped off as if she, too, had on giant black spiked boots. I shook my head and squeezed my eyes shut. It all just kept getting worse and worse, and it wasn't even Sunday.

From MY room, I could hear music so loud it made my teeth chatter.

"I'm sorry, Ben," my mom said. "It's only for a little while. I feel sorry for her."

"Aren't you going to tell her to turn off the music?"

"In a little while. I want her to settle in and feel at home. Why don't you knock on her door and see if she needs anything?"

I didn't want to do this, but I went and knocked anyway. I was surprised that Thursday let me in.

"My mom wants to know if you need any-thing," I said.

Thursday was sitting cross-legged on my bed, painting her fingernails black. "Nah, I'm good," she said. "As good as a person can be in this life. Which isn't great."

"What's that music?" I asked.

"G.O.T.H. It stands for Get On to Hades. You like?"

"Not bad, not bad," I said, because I wanted to sound cool. "You like the color black a lot, I guess." This did not sound cool, but Thursday didn't seem to mind.

"You might not like black now, because you're just a happy kid, but when you're older, say, around thirteen, you're going to like black because it will express how you feel. Your life will be miserable every day. Not just on Sundays."

"Thanks," I said.

"Maybe we can find something fun for you to do this vacation?" my mom said when I came back. She was looking up camps on the computer. "Something sports related maybe?"

"Not 4 Kids Only," I said.

"We have to have you do something, though? Won't you get bored?"

"I can play video games," I said.

"How can you play them all day? Won't it make your eyes hurt? And what will you do when I have to work? Maybe you can show Amy—uh, Thursday—around?"

Anything but that. My mom smiled at me like she could tell she'd won.

"How about this camp?" She handed me a flyer with a picture of some kids in baseball caps. SUPER SPORT BASEBALL CLEAT CAMP.

I love baseball. That chalk diamond on the green grass as the sun sets over the hills. The smell of grilled nitrate-filled hot dogs that your mom never lets you eat. Sliding into home. (Except when you're tagged out.) Mud permanently ground into your knees. (Except when you have to use a washcloth to scrub them clean in the bath.) Candy and chips with hydrogenated oils in them that your mom has to let you have because everyone else is eating them. (Except when it's her turn to be in charge of snacks and she brings tangerines and organic almonds.)

I've been in Little League for four years, and this spring will be my fifth. My problem with Little League was that if I didn't do well, I got really mad at myself and threw my glove. Then my mom came running into the dugout to talk to me, and this made everything worse. The coaches had to tell her not to interfere.

"But it's so hard for me to watch Ben that upset," my mom said.

They reassured her that they'd take care of me and made her go sit back down.

I guess her behavior kind of worked, because toward the end of the season, I'd stopped doing it just to avoid her running into the dugout with a pack of tissues.

My thing is I really, really, like to win. And I really, really, really, a hundred million *really*s, hate to lose. It makes me feel like a giant failure.

I looked at the picture of the smiling kids.

Maybe Super Sport Baseball Cleat Camp would give me an edge over the other kids in Little League when spring came.

And I didn't want to stay home with Angelina over vacation. She would torment me with Lady Blah-Blah and Dustin Peeper songs, cheers, and running around the house screaming while Monkeylad tried to lick the lotion off her legs. Plus, I got enough of her when I had to sleep in the cot in her room and asphyxiate on perfume and nail polish while Dustin Peeper watched me with his beady eyes and too much hair. Worse, I could get left with Thursday, having to show her around, having to hear her talk about how life was hell, having to listen to her music. So I said yes to my mom.

CHAPTER 9
CHRISTMAS COFFIN

My mom's new friend came by for Christmas Eve dinner with my family and Thursday.

"This is Tree," my mom said. "He's my yoga instructor. He also does acupuncture and is a nutritionist."

Our new roommate smirked. I kind of agreed with her. *Tree? Seriously?* But then I remembered that her name was Thursday.

"Your name is *Tree*?" Angelina said.

"Angelina," my mom said in the voice that means *Rude! Stop!*

"That's okay," said Tree, smiling secretively with just the corners of his lips. Tree is a skinny but muscular guy with a shaved head. "It might sound strange. My name was Daniel Zimmerman, but I changed it."

TREE

"Tree is great," my mom said. "Would you like some chicken tamales?"

"No, thank you. I brought my special delicious salad. I'm a raw foodist." Tree gave us that same smile, took a large container full of salad from his backpack, and began to pour ingredients from smaller containers onto it. "Spirulina, flaxseed oil, lemon juice, raw organic sunflower seeds, sprouted almonds . . ." He listed each thing as he put it in. My mom watched with her hands clasped together as if it was the best thing she had ever seen.

Thursday made a gagging face behind their backs and pretended to stick her finger down her throat.

"Why don't you do the dishes, kids," said Tree when Thursday, Angelina, and I were done eating tamales and Tree and my mom had eaten the raw-food salad. "I can give your mom an acupuncture treatment while you clean up."

Thursday said she was really sorry but that she was allergic to dish soap, and disappeared into her (my) room. Angelina and I just looked at each other. Even Angelina was speechless. We went into the kitchen while my mom lay on the couch. Tree stuck needles in her body. Every so often she would make little *ouch* sounds and I'd run in to see if she was okay.

"Oh, yes, it's helping a lot," my mom promised.

I didn't see how getting stuck with

sharp needles really did anything except hurt and get you out of doing the dishes.

We heard a banging sound, and I ran back in to see if Tree was doing something weird to our house, but the sound was coming from my room.

Tree knocked loudly on my door. "Excuse me, we're doing a healing session out here."

"So am I," Thursday answered without opening up. She always kept my room locked.

"Maybe it will keep her out of trouble," my mom said.

I figured the acupuncture would keep my mom out of the kitchen long enough for Angelina and me to find some sugar (maybe some old candy the Halloween Fairy had hidden?), but there wasn't any around.

Angelina and I didn't brush our teeth, take baths, or even put on our pajamas, and Mom was too busy with Tree to remind us for once. Angelina sat Monkeylad on her lap and made him "sing" a Dustin Peeper song like a ventriloquist's dummy.

" 'I love you, baby, you pretty little girl.' "

"But you're not as cute as my friend the squir-rel," I added.

This cracked us both up. I had actually made Angelina laugh!

"Angelina, can I have Monkey-lad tonight?" I asked.

"Sure."

I couldn't believe it. I got up and took Monkeylad in my arms and brought him back to my cot. He snuggled up next to me with his snout tucked into my armpit. He felt so warm.

"What do you think of Tree?" I asked my sis-ter after we'd turned off the lights. Monkeylad had started to snore softly into my armpit, and it tickled.

"What do you think I think?" she said, but she didn't sound mean like she sometimes does.

"That he's crazy, like all of Mom's friends?" I said.

"Yes," said Angelina. "How about you?"

"I think he's crazy, too," I said.

But secretly, I was kind of glad to have another guy around, since I'd never had a dad. Monkeylad and I sometimes got tired of being the men of the house. It was a pretty big responsibility.

"Can Monkeylad still sleep with me sometimes when I move back in my room?" I asked Angelina.

"We'll see," she said.

In the morning I had this tingly feeling in my stomach that might have actually been happiness. I guess that's where the expression *that Christmas-morning feeling* comes from.

I tiptoed into the living room at 5:45 A.M. The air in the house was cold, and the room smelled like pine needles from the Christmas bush. My mom said she was saving money this year by getting a bush instead of a tree.

 When she brought it home, she reminded me of Monkeylad bringing us unwanted meat: all proud and happy, and Angelina and me just staring at him like, *What the heck are you doing, please get that thing out of here.*

Beside the Christmas bush (not *under* it, because it was too short) was something wrapped awkwardly in newspaper. I could tell right away what it was.

"Mom!" I yelled. "Angelina! Monkeylad!" I couldn't even act cool. I almost wanted to call for Thursday.

My mom came in first in her red footsie pajamas that she likes to wear on Christmas, and Angelina in her Hey! Bunny Rabbit! pajamas.

"Did Santa bring you something good?" my mom asked.

I was too excited to be mad at her for talking baby talk. I started ripping off the newspaper wrapping. A brand-new red bike! When I sat on it, my knees didn't touch my elbows like with my old one. It was extremely AWESOME.

After we ate whole wheat pancakes, I asked if I could ride my new bike. My mom said, "Not by yourself. Maybe Angelina will go. Or maybe Tree will go with you later. He's really into bikes."

But Angelina wasn't going to ride bikes with me. And I didn't want Tree to go. I didn't even know him. Rocko and Leif Zuniga were probably riding bikes together around their neighborhood while their not-so-safe mothers were home watching lots of TV and eating some of the cookies they had baked for their children.

I wanted to tell my mom that it was more dangerous inside our house than outside, because there were crazy people trying to stick you with needles and creepy people in shoes with real spikes sticking out of them, ready to impale you.

I told my mom she was mean. Why couldn't she be a less safe mom?

The thing about my mom is, no matter how angry I get at her, she'll usually just hug and kiss me and tell me she loves me. And usually I let her. Angelina doesn't. When Angelina gets mad at her, my mom usually ignores it and says "I love you" and tries to hug her, and Angelina runs away screaming and crying and slamming doors. So this time, when my mom tried to hug me, I wouldn't let her. I decided to be more like Angelina, because that seemed to work out better for her.

Tree came over, and we rode bikes to the top of the hill together, and we watched the sun setting over Filmland, making the sky pink and orange and purple. You could see a thin crescent moon. The sunset was cool, and Tree was pretty nice, actually, but it wasn't the same as being with my nonexistent friends.

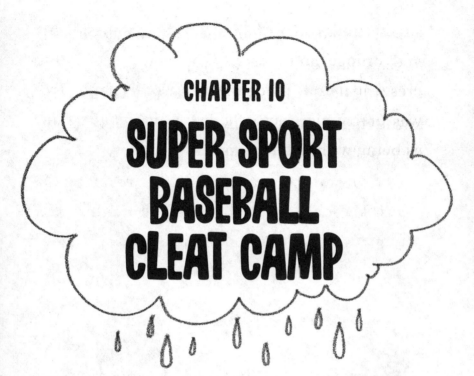

CHAPTER 10
SUPER SPORT BASEBALL CLEAT CAMP

The first day of Super Sport Baseball Cleat Camp, my mom drove me up the hill to the field. We passed the dog park, where we can never, ever take Monkeylad because he will go crazy and bark at all the other dogs until we are thrown out. We passed ladies in matching shirts, race-walking. My mom beeped the horn at them and pumped her fist in the air. "Go, ladies!" she said. I slid down in my seat. We passed the now-deserted snack bar where I'm never allowed to get a hot dog.

We parked, and my mom had to walk me over to the dugout to meet my coach, Terrence Hoof, and pay him for the camp.

A really tall man in a Genies hat was tying his cleats. He looked up and smiled at me big. His chompers made mine look small.

"You a Darters fan?"

I nodded.

"I'm a Genies guy myself." He stood up. He was *really* tall. "How's it going?" he said. "I'm Coach Hoof."

GENIES ARE LAME

I shook his hand.

"Not like that," he said. "Give me a real grip."

I tried to grab on tighter.

"That's better. What's your name?"

"Ben," I said.

"I can't hear you. What did you say?"

"Ben?" I said louder.

"You don't sound so sure. Are you not so sure what your name is?"

"Ben."

"Oh, Ben," he whispered, imitating me. "Ben, you have to raise your voice so people can hear you. Now go on and warm up."

I just stared at him.

"Go on," he said, taking off my cap and

ruffling my hair, then putting my cap back on. "Get out of here, Mr. Darter."

I ran off. I wasn't sure what I thought of this guy.

"Bye, Ben," my mom said, but I noticed she wasn't looking at me with the sad expression she has in her eyes whenever I go off to do something new. She was playing with her hair and staring at Coach Hoof the way my sister looks at her posters of Dustin Peeper.

Coach Hoof was really hard on us. He made us run up a hill until it felt like my lungs were going to pop. Then he made us do thousands of sit-ups and push-ups. My back sagged during the push-ups, and then Coach told me to put my knees down, which I refused to do because that is for wimps. I gritted my teeth so hard that my jaw pounded, and I kept doing the push-ups the real way.

All the other kids had chips and cookies and Island Mist juice drinks in their lunches, and I only got a sandwich, fruit, and water. My feet and ankles and knees hurt.

On the second morning, my heel hurt so badly I could hardly walk, but my mom made me go to camp anyway. She said it was because she didn't want to waste the money and she had to work and I could sit out if I wanted to. Coach made me run, even with a hurt heel. He said athletes had to learn to deal with pain.

On the third day, we were practicing our swings in the batting cage, and I kept missing. I threw down my glove, and Coach Hoof just ignored me and went on to the next kid. Basically, camp was eight hours of physical and mental torture. On top of that, we hardly got to play any baseball.

"There will be plenty of time for that later," Coach said. "Now we're conditioning."

The only good thing was that at the end of the day, he gave us Long Pops, and when my mom came to pick me up, she was so busy smiling at

Coach Hoof that she didn't even notice I was eating sugar on a weekday.

But the Long Pop didn't make up for the fact that a little Peeper-haired bully whose name rhymes with *socko* showed up at Super Sport Baseball Cleat Camp on the fourth day. And of course he was wearing a Genies hat.

"You've got good taste in teams, young man," Coach Hoof said when he saw Rocko Hoggen. He and Rocko high-fived. "I can tell you're a serious ballplayer. Let's see how fast you can run."

Rocko took off up the hill.

"What are you doing standing there, Darter? RUN! See if you can catch up with Genie, there."

All I could think of was 4 Kids Only and how Rocko had pushed me down and broken my clavicle.

"Go on," Coach said again. So I ran, but Rocko had a head start, and he got to the fence first.

He was standing there, smiling at me so his perfect little teeth showed. "Hey, Ben. Don't run too hard. You might fall and break something again."

I turned to Rocko Hoggen with my hand clenched into a fist, but someone was holding my arm. Someone strong.

"Okay, Darter, that's enough. Run it off," Coach Hoof said.

And I did. I tried. By the time my mom came to pick me up, I could barely walk. Her hair was all smooth and straight. She had on makeup and tight jeans and high heels. I knew this had to do with Coach Hoof. Oh, man.

At least it turned out that Rocko wasn't in camp the next day, because his family had decided to go on a last-minute trip to Hawaii. I didn't have to deal with him until school started again. But he'd managed to ruin baseball for me anyway. I decided not to sign up for Little League in the spring. I just wanted to take a break from organized activities and ride bikes with a friend. Not that *that* was going to happen either.

The day before we went back to school, Thursday left. I opened the door of my room, expecting to feel relief as soon as I was able to sink onto my mattress away from the floating, fluffy-haired faces of Dustin Peeper.

But I never made it to my bed.

Something was wrong.

Way wrong.

The walls of my room were painted as black as Thursday's eyeliner and hair and clothes, and my bed looked different, too. Someone had built a wooden lid that hinged onto my bed frame. My bed was a coffin!

How appropriate, because I wanted to curl up and die. And it was Sunday. Maybe Thursday's theory was right.

JANUARY

CHAPTER 11

CAREER DAY AKA MORTIFY BEN HUNTER DAY

I was sore from Super Sport Baseball Cleat Camp when I got back to school after winter break. I was still sharing Angelina's room because my mom hadn't had the chance to re-paint mine yet and I couldn't sleep in there with those black walls. At least Angelina sometimes let me sleep with Monkeylad. Tree had come over a few times to ride bikes with me, but I was still not allowed to ride alone.

I'd thought I'd be happy to return to school

after my miserable vacation. It seemed like even picking gum wads off the bottom of desks in Ms. Washington's class would be preferable, but then something happened to make me think winter break hadn't been so bad after all.

Today was Career Day. Another name for this should be Mortify Ben Hunter Day. When I first heard about it, I thought that real professionals who did interesting things would come, but it turned out to be just the parents. Every year my mom came to Career Day, even though I told her she shouldn't waste her time talking to a bunch of ungrateful kids who were only interested in the parents who were firefighters or police officers or the ones who worked on movies. Each year was worse because the older we got, the less interested kids were in parents who had regular, boring jobs like our resident librarian, aka my mom, who ignored my hints and came anyway.

She didn't wear her yoga pants. Instead she wore what she thought was a librarian outfit, even though she didn't actually wear that skirt and sweater to work. On Career **CAREER** **DAY!** Day she put her hair up in a bun and wore her glasses. This part was a relief because she looked a little more normal.

But then she went on and on about how important reading is and how books can change your life. She said that when you care about a character, even if they aren't perfect, and you watch them change and grow by solving problems, at the end of the novel you feel better about yourself.

Today she asked the kids in class how books can change your life. Mercy Keating raised her hand. Mercy Keating never talks in class ever.

"I love books because I used to have these scary thoughts, but when I read a book, it makes them go away."

My mom looked like she was going to run over and give Mercy Keating a kiss on the cheek.

Mercy is really short and wears tiny glasses that she could have borrowed from her Stuff-It teddy bear. She always wears the same blue turtleneck and green corduroy pants. She loves books as much as Joe Knapp does. Suddenly I had this thought that made me feel the way you do when you hit your funny bone and your whole body buzzes: my mom would rather have Mercy Keating as her kid than me.

"That's lovely, Mercy," my mom said. "That's why in my house we don't have television—so that my family can spend more time reading books."

I didn't have time to worry about Mom liking Mercy more than me; now I had to worry about all the kids who were looking at me and whispering "No TV?" and laughing, especially Rocko Hoggen.

My mom handed out library card applications to the kids who didn't have them and then left with so much pep in her step that I thought she was going to skip home.

Later, Joe Knapp's dad talked about being a veterinarian. He was a skinny guy with a long nose and droopy eyes. I thought he was pretty cool, even though he had dressed up as a baby on Halloween. He said sometimes he could communicate better with animals than with people. That animals, like people, just needed to be understood. I wondered if he could help me communicate better with Monkeylad and set him straight about not getting demon eyes and stealing the neighbors' food.

Then the next parent came in to talk to our class. He's an art director on movies. Which explained Rocko's life-size mission.

Rocko's dad talked about how he designed all this "rad" (his word) stuff, like in the movie *Incarnation*. He actually designed the digitally animated fluorescent-orange winged aliens. He showed us his sketches of them and how he worked with the director and animators to help bring his vision to life. After he was done, he gave out these bags with pictures of the aliens from the movie. Inside there was a poster, a DVD, a T-shirt, a little winged alien action figure, and some *Incarnation* candy.

Ms. Washington clapped and clapped when he was finished and thanked him about a million times.

INCARNATION
the movie

On my way out of the classroom, I saw all these yellow pieces of paper scattered on the floor. They were the library card applications from my mom. Only Mercy Keating and Joe Knapp were clutching theirs as their parents picked them up from school. Joe Knapp waved his at me in what seemed to be an actual hello, but I was too depressed to wave back.

When my mom and I took Monkeylad for his evening walk, I used the *Incarnation* bag as a poop picker-upper. I ate the candy first, of course. You can't let perfectly good candy go to waste, even if the clavicle-breaking bully's father gave it to you.

After the walk, I threw the ball for Monkeylad in the backyard. I figured he might get tired and not have demon eyes. That night Angelina let him sleep with me on my bed.

The next day we were supposed to write a letter to our favorite Career Day parent and put it in an envelope to give to them. I wrote to Joe Knapp's dad.

Dear Dr. Knapp,

Thank you for visiting our classroom on Career Day. I'm interested in what you do, because it seems like a veterinarian is someone who likes animals and is kind to them. I have a dog named Monkeylad, who sometimes acts like he's possessed by a demon. His eyes turn blue and roll back in his head, and he runs around the house in circles growling to himself. Sometimes he runs away and steals food off people's tables and brings it back as if he thinks he is doing us a favor. If you were my vet, I would ask you what to do about Monkeylad. He doesn't really obey us. We got him at the shelter as a rescue, so maybe that's why. Sometimes I think that he was not loved properly as a pup, and maybe he didn't get enough to eat, which is why he thinks he has to steal food for us.

Sincerely,

Ben Hunter

When I turned in my letter, I saw there were only two others there for Dr. Knapp. One was from Ms. Washington because she wrote to everyone.

On the way home, I peeked inside my mom's envelope. There were only three letters. One was from Joe Knapp, and one from Mercy Keating. Mercy said she wanted to be a writer when she grew up and maybe someday her books could be in a library. Joe had drawn a pretty good picture of my mom smiling and holding up a book. There was a kid in a chair next to her with really red cheeks that matched his Darters baseball cap. Probably me.

All the other letters must have been in Rocko's father's envelope.

FEBRUARY

I will not chase girls around the schoolyard.
I will not chase girls around the schoolyard.
I will not chase girls around the schoolyard.
I will not chase girls around the schoolyard.
I will not chase girls around the schoolyard.
I will not chase girls around the schoolyard.
I will not chase girls around the schoolyard.
I will not chase girls around the schoolyard.
I will not chase girls around the schoolyard.
I will not chase girls around the schoolyard.
I will not chase girls around the schoolyard.
I will not chase girls around the schoolyard.

Dear Ben,

This is not exactly a paragraph about why not to play unsupervised chasing games at recess. Please redo it. Thank you.

Ms. Washington

CHAPTER 12

THE WAR OF THE KISSES

There was a WAR going on at my school. The war was between the fifth-grade girls and the fifth-grade boys, and it started with Rocko Hoggen and Serena Perl.

On Valentine's Day—which is the absolute worst holiday ever invented, because it forces you to buy stupid stuff and makes you feel inadequate if nobody buys stupid stuff for you—Rocko and Leif were playing handball at recess and I was running around the track by myself when I saw Serena Perl skip over to them. It's weird, but I can see what she's doing no matter where she is; it's like I have a sixth sense about her. The Serena sense.

I saw her skip over and kiss Rocko on the cheek.

Yes, actually kiss him.

Although I was a ways away, it felt like Rocko had slammed the handball into my stomach. I almost doubled over.

Rocko stared at Serena. Then he dropped the ball and ran off yelling.

Serena just stood there. She was wearing a T-shirt with a puppy and red hearts on it. A lot like that valentine she had made for me in kindergarten. Her hair was in perfect braids, as usual. They bounced as she skipped away.

The next day when I was running laps around the playground, I noticed Serena heading for Rocko again. This time he noticed, too, and ran away, yelling. She followed him. Pretty soon,

five other girls—Julie Chen, Ella Bean, Aurora Richards, Kennedee Jones, and Regina Mendez— joined her, chasing Rocko while Leif tried to ward them off.

"Hey, Ben," Rocko yelled as he passed me, "you've got to help protect me from these girls."

"Yeah, Ben," said Leif, "help us."

I realized this was my chance.

My chance to join Leif in an activity, even if it involved Rocko, and, most of all, to chase down Serena Perl, though I had no idea what I would do if I caught her.

But I joined in. I caught up with Serena almost right away. All the other girls stopped behind her.

"Hey," I said, blocking her from Rocko's path.

"Hi, Ben."

"What are you doing?"

"Chasing Rocko. I'm going to kiss him."

"I don't think he wants you to," I said. "That's why he's running away. And yelling." Serena smelled like cherry candy and lip gloss. I thought of how Monkeylad chases Angelina down to lick her lip gloss off.

Serena shrugged. She suddenly looked sad. Not just her eyes, which always looked a little sad, but her whole face.

Just then the bell rang and recess was over.

Why wasn't Serena Perl chasing me? Why didn't she want to kiss me? My misery led me not only to give up on Serena Perl but to give up on myself. I became Rocko Hoggen's henchman.

Every day at recess for almost a week, the same thing happened.

Rocko and Leif would play handball, Serena Perl and her five friends would come over, and Serena would try to kiss Rocko. He and Leif would run away, and Rocko would call to me, "Hey, Ben, we could use a little help here, man," and I would run after Serena Perl. I would get in between her and Rocko Hoggen, and she and I would say hello to each other very politely and then the bell would ring.

Rocko thanked me and held up his fist to bump mine. "You're the man," he said. I had to admit, it made me feel pretty good when he said that.

But on Friday, Mr. Garcia, the PE coach, noticed what was going on. He blew his whistle just as I was taking off after Serena Perl.

"Hunter, what are you doing?"

I skidded to a stop, and Serena and her friends ran off.

It was hard to see him—the sun was blasting off the blacktop into my eyes. "Nothing, Mr. Garcia."

I couldn't see him, but I knew he was frowning. "It looked to me like you were chasing the girls. You know there are no unsupervised chasing games allowed at recess."

"Okay."

"I expect more from you, Ben Hunter," Mr. Garcia said. "You have potential as an athlete, and you're wasting it in these silly games. You're in fifth grade now. It's a whole different ball game."

"Okay."

"Okay, what?"

"Okay, Mr. Garcia?"

"Okay, you won't chase girls."

I nodded.

"And speak up. I can hardly hear you." He pointed to my Darters baseball jersey. "Do you think that guys who play for the Darters chased girls when they were in school? Or do you think they practiced to be great players from the time they were small boys?"

I thought they probably chased girls, but I couldn't really say that. "Okay, sorry?"

"Don't speak in questions. Say it like you mean it. I'll have to speak to your teacher about this."

No! I didn't want him to tell Ms. Washington. She would think I was becoming a troublemaker.

"Ben, what happened?" she asked when I got back to class.

I shrugged.

"Were you chasing Serena at recess?"

I nodded and slumped into my Darters jersey. It was too hard to explain. What could I say? That I was trying to impress Leif Zuniga? That I was defending my enemy from being kissed by Serena Perl? That I did it to be closer to her?

Ms. Washington leaned closer. "You like Serena, right, Ben?"

I looked up into her eyes. For the first time, I realized her face reminded me of the pop star Nananna except with glasses. I didn't say anything.

"I get it. She's a nice girl. Just please don't chase her. You can go up to her and say hello if you want to talk to her. I need you to write a paragraph about it, please."

She handed me a piece of paper and touched my shoulder before she walked away.

At recess the next day, Joe Knapp was doing laps around the playground. He wasn't very fast, and he was breathing hard. I slowed down so he could catch up. His legs looked super skinny in his shorts, and he had a Timmy the Train bandage on his knee, poor kid.

"Hi," he said.

"Hi."

"Wanna play handball?" he asked.

"Sure," I said.

"I saw what happened with Rocko Hoggen and Serena."

"Oh, yeah?"

"He's the one who should've gotten in trouble."

While Joe Knapp and I played handball, we had a man-to-man talk.

"Do you like Serena?" Joe asked me as he tried to hit the ball down with both fists and his butt sticking out.

I caught the ball and held it in my hand, pointed to Joe and then to the ball. Then I slammed it against the wall with one fist. "Like this," I said.

He nodded and rubbed his eyes behind his glasses. "Because I like Aurora Richards."

Aurora Richards is the oldest and tallest kid in our class, and Joe is the youngest and shortest. Aurora is one of those December birthday kids who stayed back a year. Aurora Richards looks like a little Hellwig Plum, that model who hosts *America's Next OMG*. There is no way in hellwig that she would like Joe Knapp.

"Oh, cool," I said.

"I mean, I really like her," Joe said, catching the ball in both hands and staring at it as if it were Aurora Richards. "Even her name is perfect. It means *dawn*, and it also means lights in the sky in high-latitude regions caused by a collision of atoms and particles in the thermosphere."

Huh? That Joe Knapp is quite a character. I took the ball gently from his hands. "Yeah. I've liked Serena Perl since kindergarten."

"Wow," Joe Knapp said. "Maybe she likes you, too. But she just doesn't want to admit it, so she chases Rocko."

For one second I felt this warmth expanding inside my chest. Joe and I stood there looking at each other. I could tell by his little puppy eyes behind the smeared lenses of his glasses that he understood.

"Hit it like this," I said, slamming the ball with my fist.

Joe Knapp clasped his hands together and swung lightly, hitting the ball directly back at the wall with only a slight lift of his butt.

"Good job, man," I said. "But you need to tell your mom to get you a different bandage. Timmy the Train will get you laughed out of class."

Joe Knapp nodded and smiled. He still had baby teeth, more than I did. You gotta love that little kid.

We high-fived.

"Hey, I could use your help on something, too," I said.

"Sure," said Joe.

"Remember when I chased Serena around the yard for Rocko? Ms. Washington wants me to write an essay on why that's not cool, and I know she's right, but for some reason I can't think of what to write."

"Maybe you did it because you want Serena and Rocko to like you. And you chose Rocko over Serena because she was chasing him instead of you."

That about summed it up.

MARCH

WHY IT'S NOT A GOOD IDEA TO PLAY UNSUPERVISED CHASING GAMES AT RECESS
by Ben Hunter

I'm sorry for the incident involving an unsupervised chasing game at recess. I believe I did this because I wanted to be liked by my classmates, but in the end, the classmate I wanted to like me the most was the one who could've gotten hurt. I will do my best to refrain from committing such a reprehensible action in the future.

The reason this should not happen again is that it could interrupt other students who are having a peaceful recess. Also, fellow students could fall and scrape their faces off.

In addition, I could fall and scrape my face off.

This behavior will not happen again, because we want to keep our faces on our face.

CHAPTER 13
SPELLING BEE'S KNEES

In March we had a spelling bee. Ms. Washington called it "the Spelling Bee's Knees."

Everyone else messed up on their words except Rocko and me. We stood at the front of the classroom under the hanging solar system and in front of the instructions on how to write an essay. Rocko and I were supposed to each spell three words at a time until someone messed up.

Ms. Washington picked a word out of the basket.

"Rocko, how do you spell *able*? Use it in a sentence, please."

"Able. *A-B-L-E*. Some people are able to beat others to the fence in Super Sport Baseball Cleat Camp, and they are also able to go to Hawaii for vacation."

I clenched my fist under the table.

"Correct," Ms. Washington said, reaching into the basket. "Now please spell *fragile*."

"Fragile. *F-R-A-G-I-L-E*. Some people's bones are more fragile than other people's bones."

I bit my lip, which can be dangerous when your front teeth are as big as mine.

"Correct, Rocko," said Ms. Washington, picking another word. "And now please spell *temper*."

"Temper. *T-E-M-P-E-R*. Some people have a bad temper and try to hit you when you ask them if they had a nice winter break."

"Okay, very good. Now it's Ben's turn. Ben, how do you spell *detrimental*?" Ms. Washington asked. "And please put it in a sentence." She smiled at me like a movie star on the red carpet, all proud, as if she expected me to rock this one.

I looked at Rocko and thought about my broken clavicle that had probably healed crooked and would never be a normal clavicle again. "Detrimental. *D-E-T-R-I-M-E-N-T-A-L*. Some people are detrimental to my health."

"Correct. How do you spell *treachery*?"

Easy peasy. "Treachery. *T-R-E-A-C-H-E-R-Y*. Breaking someone's collarbone may be considered treachery."

Ms. Washington smiled at me with her big brown eyes, very much like bigger, darker versions of the eyes of Serena Perl, who, incidentally, was looking not at me but at Rocko Hoggen.

"Your last word, Ben, is *teachable*."

Maybe I was distracted by Serena Perl, but all of a sudden, I just saw these letters playing a crazy basketball game in front of my eyes, bouncing all around in a blur. "Teachable. *T-E-A-C-H-A-B-E-L*. We try to train my dog, Monkeylad, but he's not teachable."

Ms. Washington looked sad, with all the usually upward-turning parts of her face turning down.

"I'm sorry, Ben. That's not correct. Rocko?"

"Teachable. *T-E-A-C-H-A-B-L-E*," said Rocko Hoggen. "Some people misspell words and are not teachable."

Everyone laughed. Including Leif Zuniga and Serena Perl.

"That's enough, Rocko."

"Sorry, Ben," he said. He actually sounded like he meant it.

"Good work, boys." Ms. Washington held up a medal with a picture of a bee on it and pinned it on Rocko Hoggen. "Congratulations. You're the bee's knees. Okay, class, time for recess."

Ms. Washington asked me to stay and talk to her—"Ben, Ben, please"—but I was already running outside as fast as I could go.

Unfortunately, you can't outrun everything.

Ella Bean and Regina Mendez joined me. I

slowed down to be nice when they called my name. Big mistake.

"Hi, Ben," they said.

"Hi."

"Can we have your Darters jersey?" Regina asked.

"Sorry, no."

"But we want it. It's cool." They started to chase me, so I ran fast.

"I bet he'd give it to Serena if she asked," Ella said.

"Hey, Ben," Regina yelled after me, "Serena told me she doesn't like you. At all. Not even as a friend."

Have I mentioned that my life is miserable?

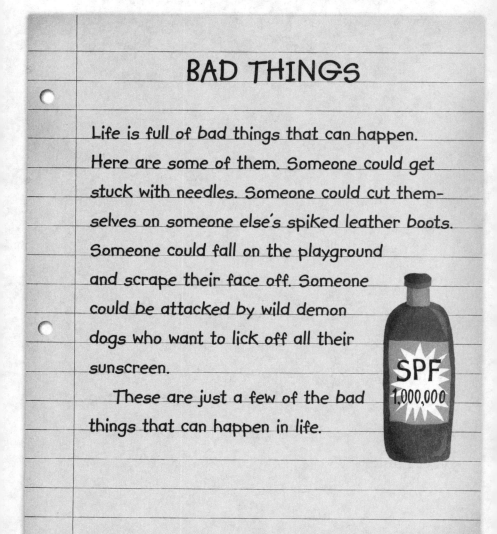

BAD THINGS

Life is full of bad things that can happen. Here are some of them. Someone could get stuck with needles. Someone could cut themselves on someone else's spiked leather boots. Someone could fall on the playground and scrape their face off. Someone could be attacked by wild demon dogs who want to lick off all their sunscreen.

These are just a few of the bad things that can happen in life.

SPF 1,000,000

CHAPTER 14
REAL-LIFE MONSTERS

Ms. Washington took me aside at recess the next day.

"Ben, I want to talk to you."

"Uh, okay."

"Is everything all right at home?"

I was so frustrated that I just started talking. I couldn't stop. I told Ms. Washington about all the things that had been bothering me since Christmas. Tree and Thursday and camp and my bike. I don't know if I made any sense. But I didn't tell Ms. Washington about the thing that was bothering me the most: Serena Perl.

"Maybe we should have a conference with your mom," Ms. Washington said.

The next day my mom came in.

"Ben seems a little upset," Ms. Washington began as we sat in the kid chairs in my classroom that made my mom's and Ms. Washington's knees come up too high. "He said something about a girl who painted his room black."

"I know," said my mom. "I feel terrible. My friend's daughter came to stay with us over Christmas, and she'd changed a lot. She painted Ben's room. And she nailed something to his bed."

"Made my bed into a coffin," I said.

My mom looked very upset. "We dismantled that, but I haven't had a chance to repaint, so Ben's been staying with his sister until we do." She looked at me. "I'm sorry, Ben."

"Ben also said something about needles?"

"Oh, yes. That must have worried you. Acupuncture needles," my mom said. "My friend Tree has been giving me acupuncture, which has helped a lot. I tend to get a little anxious."

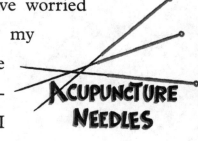

ACUPUNCTURE NEEDLES

"Ben, is there anything else you want to talk about?" Ms. Washington asked.

Not Serena Perl! But I did think about mentioning my bike. "No," I said.

"It would be great to talk about how you are feeling. Are you sure?"

I nodded but wouldn't look at Ms. Washington.

My mom was really quiet on the way home. When we got there, she said, "Your teacher did the right thing calling me in, Ben. I want you to know that you can always talk to me about anything."

I thought about my shiny new bike. All I wanted was to ride it by myself in the fresh air and let the wind blow the day out of my head, let

 my legs pedal away the stress. Even though Tree had come over to ride with me a few times, it wasn't enough. And I still felt a little awkward with him.

"Why won't you let me ride my bike by myself!" I shouted at my mom.

She sat down next to me. "Ben, I have to explain something to you. There's a reason I won't let you ride your bike alone. And it isn't because I'm mean."

"No, it's because you are a safe mom!" I shouted, like it was the worst insult I could think of. Except to mention her messy hair and yoga pants, which seemed a little below the belt.

"I think it's time for me to be straight with you, Ben. I don't want to scare you, but there are dangerous people out there."

"I know that," I said. She had already told me you shouldn't talk to strangers and that some people weren't safe. Hello. I mean, she was the one who had allowed the needles and spikes to come into our home. "That's why you should get me a cell phone! Have you ever thought of that? Angelina has one."

"She's older and walks to school with Amanda Panda. When you're in middle school, you can have a phone. The radiation is not good for growing brains, and the only reason I let your sister have one is for emergencies."

"I want to be able to walk to school alone! And ride my bike to school! Emergencies? Angelina texts all day about what outfit she's going to wear. Is that an emergency?"

My mom didn't seem to hear me. "There was a little boy who got lost on his way home from school. His parents had let him go by himself for the first time. They had practiced with him, and they were nervous, but they let him go."

"So what?" I said. I was so mad, it felt like my heart was the rubber one on Rocko's Halloween costume—not my lame costume, but the cool one that spurted blood.

"And someone kidnapped him," she said.

I felt like when I broke my collarbone, except I felt it in every bone of my body. "They kidnapped him?"

"Yes," said my mom.

"How old was he?"

"Nine."

"Did they ever find him?"

"No."

I thought about this little kid walking home, all proud of himself, excited to see his parents and celebrate with them and then getting lost and someone, some big monster, grabbing him and then his parents waiting and waiting and worrying and then calling the police and not hearing from him. I was so scared and sad and mad I couldn't express all those things, and there was only one person to take it out on. So I tried to hit my mom.

"I hate you," I said. "I hate your hair and your

clothes and the lunches you pack me and your boring house and your safeness!"

I had never tried to hit my mother before.

She held my arms down and pulled me to her. "I'm sorry, Ben. I'm sorry, baby."

"Don't call me baby," I said.

"I'm sorry, Ben. I didn't mean to scare you."

"I'm not scared," I said. "I just hate you for being so safe."

"I know. And I love you," she said.

I hate my mom, even if she is just trying to protect me. And my new bike that I almost NEVER GET TO RIDE. Rocko Hoggen. Leif Zuniga. Even Serena Perl. And especially the monster that kidnapped that little kid.

And I hate myself because I came along and made Angelina jealous and my mom worried. My life is miserable, and I realize now it's my own miserable fault.

CHAPTER 15
TROUBLE

Today I got in big trouble.

Maybe it's the worst trouble I have ever gotten in. Ms. Washington gave me this freaked-out look, as if I'd hit Rocko Hoggen in the teeth.

My teacher put her hand firmly on my shoulder and walked me out to meet my mom after school. "I think we need to have another conference," she said, handing the paper I had written to my mom.

Mom read it, and I saw tears in her eyes. She

looked at me. "Ben?" she said. "Why did you write this?"

I looked at my shoes. One was untied, but I didn't bother to fix it.

We walked back to the classroom and sat down. Everyone was very quiet.

"What's this about, Ben?" Ms. Washington asked.

I shrugged.

"You don't feel okay about yourself?"

I shrugged again.

"Because you're smart and handsome and very good at sports," said Ms. Washington.

"I tell him that all the time," my mom said. She looked at me. "Don't I, Ben?"

I shook my head. "You just tell me how worried you are about me."

"Well, I think it all the time. How wonderful you are. How smart and handsome and athletic and wonderful I think you are," my mom said. "Don't you know that?"

I shrugged.

Ms. Washington said, "Ben, are you still upset about Rocko?"

I nodded.

"Because there are so many kids who like you. I know Leif likes you, even though I think he feels obligated to hang out with Rocko. And I know Joe Knapp likes you. And Serena."

"Regina said that Serena doesn't like me even as a friend," I mumbled.

Ms. Washington asked me to repeat that two times because she couldn't hear me. Each time I said it in a softer, more mumbled voice. But finally she understood me. She said, "I think Regina would only say something like that because she has a crush on you. I've seen her looking at you, and once I saw a note she wrote about it to Ella."

I looked up for a second at Ms. Washington and then I looked back down.

"So I want you to write something for me," Ms. Washington said. "I want you to write some things that are awesome about you, okay?"

I nodded. But I didn't feel ready to do that yet.

Later that day, my mom said, "Ben, let's get on our bikes and take a ride."

"Are you sure?" I asked. My mom hadn't ridden her bike in years.

"Yes. Tree has been helping me learn again. They say you never forget how to ride a bike, but that's not exactly true."

Everything looked clean after the rain. The sun was out, but it was still cold, and it made the leaves on the trees sparkle like the shiny things on Serena Perl's shirts. My bike had a fast, smooth ride. We came home, and my mom made grilled chicken burritos with guacamole for dinner.

"Mom," I said, "I'm sorry I said I hated you."

"It's okay, Ben."

She came and knelt on the kitchen floor and put her arms around me. She looked into my eyes, and it was hard for me to look into hers without giggling, even though nothing was funny.

"I know that what I said scared you. I probably

shouldn't have said it. I was just feeling like you were ready to be independent, and you can't be unless you understand how dangerous the world is. I'm so sorry it has to be that way."

"I'm sorry, Mommy," I said. And then I started to cry. I was crying for that little boy who was never found, mostly, and because I had told my mom I hated her, and because it sucks that you can't ride bikes by yourself when you're ten. My grandma said she used to ride all around the neighborhood by herself when she was my age and didn't have to come in until it got dark. But she's kind of old. It would feel good to be free like that, riding in the wind, feeling the sweat dry on your face, smelling the trees and not being afraid.

"Will I ever be able to ride my bike by myself?" I asked my mom after I had stopped crying.

"Of course you will."

But I didn't really believe her.

That night as my sister and I lay in our beds

in the dark, I saw a little light shining under Angelina's covers. She was texting, of course, even though she was supposed to have her phone off an hour before bedtime.

My mom knocked on the door like she had X-ray eyes. "Is that phone still on?"

"Oh my God, Mom, no," Angelina said.

"Because if it is, I'm going to come take it away."

Angelina turned off the phone and whispered, "I can't believe her."

"Right? She still won't even let me ride by myself."

"It's ridiculous."

We were quiet for a while. Then my sister asked me how fifth grade was.

"It's not so great," I said. Angelina had let me have Monkeylad, and he was making little piggy sounds in his sleep.

"Fifth grade was the worst," Angelina said. "I always thought I looked terrible and my hair was bad. I didn't have any real friends."

"Really?" I had no idea that my pretty, popular sister had ever felt that way.

"Yeah, that was before cheerleading and good hair products with argan oil. Middle school is way better."

"Ugh," I said.

"Don't worry, little bro. I'll hook you up. I'll still be there, and I'll tell you exactly how to dress and where to hang out at lunch. You're going to do fine. You're way smarter than I am."

I couldn't believe she was saying that. She was the one who'd talked in twelve-word sentences before she was a year old.

"Plus, you're cute. Amanda Panda and Twinkle Knoll both told me they think you're adorable and that you're going to be hot when you grow up."

I went to sleep with Monkeylad snoring softly into my armpit.

The next night before bed, my mom let Monkeylad out in the backyard. He was out there longer than usual, and then we heard him barking and barking and my mom calling and calling, her voice getting more and more shrill.

Angelina and I looked at each other in the mirror as we brushed our teeth. Why couldn't Monkeylad enjoy the night a little longer? My mom had to control all of us all the time.

Then I heard her screaming, "Ben. Angelina! Come here right now. I need your help."

My mom's voice sounded deeper. She was saying each word like it was its own sentence. I knew something was really wrong, so I went to see what was going on while Angelina ignored her and kept brushing her teeth.

"Get the flashlight. Right now," my mom said. She was standing in the yard clapping her hands and calling Monkeylad, who was still barking like crazy, and I knew she wasn't messing around. So I got the flashlight. My mom shined a beam of light over to where Monkeylad was barking. I could see a weird little-old-man face with a long pointed snout hiding among the roots of a tree.

"What is that?" I said, shuddering.

"Call Monkeylad," my mom said, keeping the little snouted thing in the beam of light. "He won't come to me."

"Monkeylad," I said, "come have a treat!"

And he came right to me. I picked him up, but he smelled stinky.

"Good job. Go inside," my mom said.

She backed into the house, and Angelina came out of the bathroom. "What stinks?" she said.

"Monkeylad got squirted by a possum," said my mom. "But Ben rescued him before anything worse happened. We need to give him a bath."

It turns out possums aren't that dangerous, but they have fifty very, very sharp teeth, and when they are scared, they squirt a stinky smell at you. Not as bad as skunk stink, but still. So I guess my mom was right to be worried about Monkeylad and to want him to come inside. I helped her give him a bath, and that night Angelina didn't even argue about letting him sleep with me.

I am not stupid and ugly and bad at sports.
I am not stupid and ugly and bad at sports.
I am not stupid and ugly and bad at sports.
I am not stupid and ugly and bad at sports.
I am not stupid and ugly and bad at sports.
I am not stupid and ugly and bad at sports.
I am not stupid and ugly and bad at sports.
I am not stupid and ugly and bad at sports.
I am not stupid and ugly and bad at sports.
Okay, did I write it enough times?

Ben,
Please rewrite this. I'd like you to tell me the
things you are, such as smart, handsome, and
athletic, as well as a very kind person. ☺

Sincerely,
Ms. Washington

I AM NOT STUPID
AND UGLY
AND BAD AT SPORTS.

CHAPTER 16

BEN HUNTER IS THE CATERPILLAR'S SPATS

Today when I came to school, Ms. Washington announced, "We're going to do a special project. Every day, one of you will get up in front of the class, and the rest of us will take turns writing on the board one thing about you that we admire." I slid down in my chair. *Awesome but embarrassment-inducing Ms. Washington, please don't call on me.*

"Ben," Ms. Washington said.

I didn't move.

"Ben, please come to the front of the class."

I got up and walked slowly from my desk. I was pretty sure my face was red because of how hot it felt. The solar system planets hanging on strings from the ceiling spun around and made me dizzy.

"Ella Bean," Ms. Washington said, "please begin."

Ella Bean walked up, took some chalk, and wrote BEN HUNTER IS WAY SMART. Then she sat down. I cringed, waiting for laughter. But no one laughed.

Kennedee Jones wrote BEN HUNTER IS A FAST RUNNER.

Aurora Richards wrote I LIKE BEN HUNTER'S EYES.

Regina Mendez wrote BEN HUNTER IS CUTE. What? I didn't know Regina Mendez thought that. It was nice, but I cringed again, and this time there were a few giggles. Then it was over and Ms. Washington called on Mercy Keating, who wrote BEN HUNTER'S MOM HAS AN INTEREST-ING JOB.

Joe Knapp wrote BEN HUNTER IS MY FRIEND IN THIS CLASS, AND HE IS THE MAN.

Leif Zuniga wrote BEN HUNTER IS A GOOD ATHLETE.

Rocko Hoggen wrote BEN HUNTER IS A TEACH-ABLE SPELLER WHEN HE IS NOT INTIMADATED.

This time everyone laughed, but I think they were laughing at Rocko's spelling.

The last person Ms. Washington called on was Serena Perl. She came up to the front of the

class, turned, looked straight at me as if she was thinking about something, smiled, turned back, and wrote BEN HUNTER IS AWESOME. OH, AND I THINK HE LIKES DOGS! Then she sat down.

"Thank you, class," Ms. Washington said. "Everyone will get a turn. And a special thanks to the parent who helped come up with this exercise. She didn't want her identity to be revealed, but maybe you can guess." She looked at me and winked.

Just then, my mom walked into the classroom.

"Oh, hi, Ms. Hunter," Ms. Washington said.

"I just wanted to stop by and see if I could help with anything. I brought some supplies from the Lurning Bush." She held up a bag of fuzzy pencils and those Japanese erasers in the shapes of cars, food, and little animals. The kids in my class love those erasers, especially the girls. I wasn't thrilled about the cute animal ones, but no one seemed to think they were a problem. The girls were really excited, squirming in their seats like they had to pee.

"Oh, thank you," said Ms. Washington, looking kind of surprised and confused. "I didn't expect you."

"I also brought some cupcakes," my mom said. "They're made with real sugar and butter and white flour." She smiled at me and held up a large pink cake box. I guess most bakeries insist on pink cake boxes. No one seemed to mind this either.

"Would you like to help pass out the erasers and cupcakes?" Ms. Washington asked me.

"Sure," I said.

"Thank you, Ben. You are the caterpillar's spats." She went over to the board and wrote BEN HUNTER IS THE CATERPILLAR'S SPATS. I'm not sure what that means, but I think she meant it as a good thing. "Would you like to ask two friends to help you?"

"Joe Knapp and Serena Perl," I said. Mercy Keating was staring at my mom like she was the Japanese eraser Mercy wanted the most. Or one shaped like a book if that was an option.

While we were eating the cupcakes, my mom went over to the board and wrote I LOVE BEN HUNTER SO MUCH THAT IF THERE WAS A LOVE METER, IT WOULD REGISTER SO HIGH IT WOULD EXPLODE.

Everyone laughed. Great. Thanks, Mom. But

the cupcakes were good, and Serena Perl liked her Japanese eraser. It was shaped like a puppy. She said she would never actually erase anything with it so the puppy wouldn't get worn out.

When I got home that afternoon (which was not a Thursday), the girl Thursday was in my room on a stepladder, painting the walls white. The room smelled like paint fumes, and music was blasting.

"Hey," Thursday said when she saw me.

"Hey," I said.

Her hair was a little longer and dyed pink, and she had on a pair of light blue cutoffs and a lavender T-shirt. She wore less makeup, and I could see a few freckles on her nose. She actually looked kind of pretty. Her eyes were green, which I hadn't noticed before.

She stepped off the stepladder, put her hands on her hips, and looked at me.

"I'm sorry I painted your room black."

I noticed that the black paint was still showing through the white paint.

"Black paint is hard to cover," she said, reading my mind. "Just like the way we try to cover up the dark side of life. But you can't give up trying. Darkness is real, but so is light."

Wow, she had really changed. Maybe it was because her hair was pink? She told me that her new look was "pastel goth." So probably her hair was dyed pink because she was feeling better and not the other way around.

"No prob." She went back to painting, and I took a brush and helped her, because in some ways, she was kind of cool.

My mom ordered pizza for dinner that night, and Thursday stayed and even helped Mom set the table. Tree came by with his salad. And just as we were about to sit down, there was a knock on the door. Grandma! She had brought homemade cookies and a large container of ice cream.

"Ben!" she said, hugging me. She smelled like

honey graham crackers and vanilla and roses. "How is my adorable, wonderful young man? I love you so much. Oh, how I've missed you!"

She sat next to me, and we fed Monkeylad snacks under the table. But somehow, when we weren't looking, he must have escaped, because there was another knock on the door and the Grump was standing there with Monkeylad on a leash.

"He tried to eat my dinner again!" the Grump shouted. "But this time I caught the little monster!"

"Oh, I'm so sorry," said my grandma. "Please forgive us. Maybe you could join us for dinner, Mr. . . . Oh, please remind me of your name. I find myself forgetting things lately."

The Grump paused and frowned at her. Then he said, "Mr. Fishnik. Frank Fishnik."

No wonder he'd never told us his name. But leave it to Grandma to get it out of him.

"Oh, please come in, Mr. Fishnik. I had a friend with that same last name from the Midwest. Are you from the Midwest?" She kept talking and talking, and pretty soon he was sitting at our table eating pizza with us. My grandmother is a miracle worker.

After dinner Grandma suggested we play charades. There was no way anyone else in the world could have gotten cooler-than-thou Angelina and even-cooler-than-that Thursday and the grumpy Grump to play. But Grandma did.

My mom got Get On to Hades, Angelina got the Darters, my grandma got *Incarnation*, Thursday got Hellwig Plum, Tree got the Dustin Peeper song "I Love You, Baby, You Pretty Little Girl," and the Grump got Hey! Bunny Rabbit! You could see they were all struggling because they didn't know what they were acting out. Especially the Grump. I couldn't tell what charade he'd come up with. Maybe he was a closet

Hellwig Plum fan. I got *How to Be a Hottie*, which I had seen once at my grandma's. I nailed it when I walked like the host, Tawny Money, and everyone laughed—even Thursday, who never laughs. But I didn't mind, because they were laughing with me, not at me, since I was laughing, too.

MAY

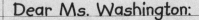

Dear Ms. Washington:

I am smart, handsome, athletic, and a good speller. I am smart, handsome, athletic, and a good speller. I am smart, handsome, athletic, and a good speller. I am smart, handsome, athletic, and a good speller. I am smart, handsome, athletic, and a good speller. I am smart, handsome, athletic, and a good speller. I am smart, handsome, athletic, and a good speller. I am smart, handsome, athletic, and a good speller. I am smart, handsome, athletic, and a good speller. I am smart, handsome, athletic, and a good speller. Oh, yeah, I am also kind and a good friend. I think Joe is getting awesome at handball. He just needs a little more confidence to realize that.

Is this better? Thank you for helping me. You are the best teacher in the whole universe.

Sincerely,
Ben Hunter

Dear Ben,

It's such a pleasure to have you in class. I've learned a lot from you. Sometimes life can be hard, can't it? But you have a lot of people who love and believe in you, and I can see that you believe in yourself more now, too. I'm going to miss you when you go to middle school. Please come visit me.

Yours truly,
Ms. Washington

CHAPTER 17
CRAZY HAT DAY

Today was crazy hat day. Last night my mom told me she'd heard me talking in my sleep. She ran into the room.

"Ben? Ben, what's wrong?"

"Don't make me wear the butterfly hat!" I'd said. But I don't remember saying it.

My mom had promised that I didn't have to, and I went back to sleep.

In the morning I put on my Darters cap because that's as crazy as I get in the hat department.

Serena Perl wore a red beanie decorated with black dots and antennae to look like a ladybug. After school they were selling Long Pops, and when my mom came to pick me up, she'd brought a dollar bill and told me I could get one for me and one for a friend.

Serena Perl was standing behind me in line. I asked her if I could buy her a Long Pop, and she said sure. We walked out together licking our pops. It made our tongues neon red. I told her that was my favorite color, and she said it was hers, too. My mom was waiting by the front gate with Monkeylad in his Halloween costume.

"I thought he might behave better in his hot-dog bun," my mom said, "even though it's not Halloween."

I bent down to pet him, and he kissed my face like a maniac.

"Oh, wow, he loves you so much!" Serena said. "Does he sleep with you? If I had a dog, I'd always want him to sleep with me."

"Sometimes," I said. "My sister and I share him." This was actually true. Angelina had started letting me have Monkeylad every other night.

My mom had brought some Chix Stix with her, and she asked Serena Perl if she would like to see Monkeylad do a trick.

"Do you want to hold up the treat for him?" my mom asked.

Serena did, and Monkeylad jumped to get it but then settled down onto his haunches and just sat like a little man. After she gave him the Chix Stix, he still sat there. And sat there some more.

"I love dogs," Serena said. "I want to be a veterinarian."

I hadn't known that about her. How could I not have known? Although she had written her Career Day thank-you note to Dr. Knapp, and she did have a lot of shirts with dogs on them.

"He's still sitting there!" Serena said.

"Would you like to come over and hang out with us sometime?" my mom said.

"Sure. That would be great. See you later, Ben. Thanks for the Long Pop."

She walked away, and Monkeylad fell onto his front paws. He looked exhausted from sitting up for so long. That couldn't have been easy, with a hard curly monkey tail like that under your bony butt.

My mom smiled at me. "Monkeylad, you little Chix magnet," she said. She held up another Chix Stix and gave it to him. "Get it, Ben, a Chix magnet?"

Then she took something out of her purse. Something dreaded that should not appear in public at any time in a kid's life. "Ben, I think you need to reapply some sunscreen before we go home. Monkeylad licked it all off you!"

"Seriously, Mom? Seriously? There is no way I'm putting that on now."

She didn't make me. Even she realized how embarrassing that would be.

Later that night, while Angelina was at Twinkle Knoll's, I asked my mom if we could watch a movie together.

"Sure," she said. "That sounds like fun." She'd been more relaxed lately. Maybe it was because she hung out with Tree and meditated and got acupuncture.

I picked a DVD of this movie *Scaranormal Activity* that Thursday had left in my room. It was supposed to be funny but also pretty scary. I showed the cover to my mom.

"No way," she said.

"Please, Mom."

She thought about it for a

minute. "I don't know. I don't want you to have nightmares."

"If it gets too scary for me, I'll let you know," I said. "And we can eat chocolate to comfort us." Angelina had convinced my mom to buy us real, sugar-sweetened chocolate eggs for Easter, and we had a few left over since, luckily, there is no Easter Fairy who steals chocolate. But we were supposed to have the chocolate eggs only on weekends, which actually just meant Saturday night, and this was a Friday.

My mom laughed. "Okay," she said. "But you have to tell me the truth. If you get too scared, we're turning it off."

So we got the chocolate eggs and sat down to watch the movie with Monkeylad sleeping on my  feet. The movie got pretty scary, and at one point, without looking away from the screen, I took my mom's arm and draped it over my shoulders.

"Are you okay?" she asked. "Should we turn it off?"

I bit into another chocolate egg without moving my eyes from the movie. "No," I said. "It's the best thing I've ever seen!"

After I finished my chocolate eggs, Monkeylad jumped up and sat in my lap, and that made me feel less scared, too.

When the movie was over, my mom admitted she'd liked it, and we talked about what made it good.

"I cared about Scary Gary," I said. "He was intrepid in the beginning, which made me like him, but it also got him in trouble, which was good for the story."

"Good use of the word *intrepid*, Ben. He changed and grew, just like in a good book," Mom said. "Maybe we'll go to the library tomorrow and find you some funny, scary novels."

I told her that sounded like a cool idea.

Intrepid

CHAPTER 18
A PERFECT DAY FOR BEN HUNTER

Tree and I have been riding our bikes to see the sunset. He's actually a pretty good guy. He told my mom I'm a really safe bike rider. I told her I had a friend to ride bikes with and could he come over so we could ride together. She finally said yes!

Today Joe Knapp came over. Turns out he loves bike riding as much as I do. His dad, the vet, dropped him off and communicated with Monkeylad. Dr. Knapp said that Monkeylad was probably traumatized in the shelter, just like I thought, and that the best thing for him was lots of exercise and slow socialization with very gentle, older dogs. Monkeylad was almost as obsessed with Dr. Knapp as with Serena Perl. My dog went right up on his haunches and just stared at Dr. Knapp for what seemed like minutes on end.

After Dr. Knapp left, Joe and I went for a ride through the neighborhood. The trees were

blooming with pinkish-purple flowers, and the air was warm and smelled almost as good as cupcakes. Joe and I rode to Serena Perl's. She got on her red bike with the glittery seat, and we all rode together around the park. Then we rode to Bigbucks coffeehouse and got chocolate Big Wippucinos. My mom even gave me money for one. She says she's trying to be less strict.

When we rode home, the warm breeze was in my face, blowing the worries of the world right out of me.

JUNE

WHAT I LEARNED IN ELEMENTARY SCHOOL

A Graduation Speech
by Ben Hunter

I learned a lot during my years in elementary school. When I started, I was just a little pipsqueak. I was excited and scared at the same time. I wanted to make friends and play, and learn cursive and math. Now, as I look back, I realize that as important as my teachers' assignments were, the things I learned about life from my teachers, especially Ms. Washington, and from my family, friends, and frenemies were even more important.

One thing I learned is to be nice to other people. Even when they make you mad. Usually they're not really trying to be mean. They're just thinking about themselves. Or sometimes, like with parents (and a shout-out to my mom here), they love you and are only trying to take care of you, even if they drive you crazy.

The second thing I learned is that if someone is being mean, you can find someone else to hang out with—"Go where the love is," like my sister, Angelina, says.

Another thing I learned is that you have to be nice to yourself. Maybe you have to be nicer to yourself when other people aren't nice to you. Don't be too hard on yourself. Life is hard enough.

But there are great things to look forward to. Like dogs, even when they act crazy, and baseball, even when you strike out, and watching scary movies with your mom while eating chocolate, and riding your bike with your best friend. I wish everyone a great summer full of all the things you love to do and only a few of the things you don't. See you in middle school!

F. L. BLOCK is the author of many award-winning and bestselling books for teens and adults.

EDWARD HEMINGWAY is the creator of *Field Guide to the Grumpasaurus, Bad Apple: A Tale of Friendship*, and *Bad Apple's Perfect Day*. He has written features for *GQ* magazine and comics for Nickelodeon, and his artwork has been published in *The New York Times* and *Nickelodeon Magazine*. He lives in Brooklyn, New York.

edward-hemingway.squarespace.com